A Dangerous Game

Tales of War book 3

Also by John Wilson

A Dangerous Game

Tales of War book 3

John Wilson

A Dangerous Game is a work of historical fiction. Reference to actual places, events and persons are used fictitiously. All other places, events and characters are the products of the author's imagination and any resemblance to actual places, events or persons is purely coincidental.

Library and Archives Canada Cataloguing in Publication

Wilson, John (John Alexander), 1951 -

A Dangerous Game/John Wilson

ISBN (paperback) 978-1-990483-08-0

ISBN (kindle) 978-1-990483-07-3

A Dangerous Game first published by Doubleday Canada, 2016

Cover design by John Wilson

Cover photography by John Wilson

For more information on the author and his books, visit:

http://www.johnwilsonauthor.com

For Violette Szabo, a real spy from the Second World War, who, at age twenty-three, was executed at Ravensbrück concentration camp in February 1945.

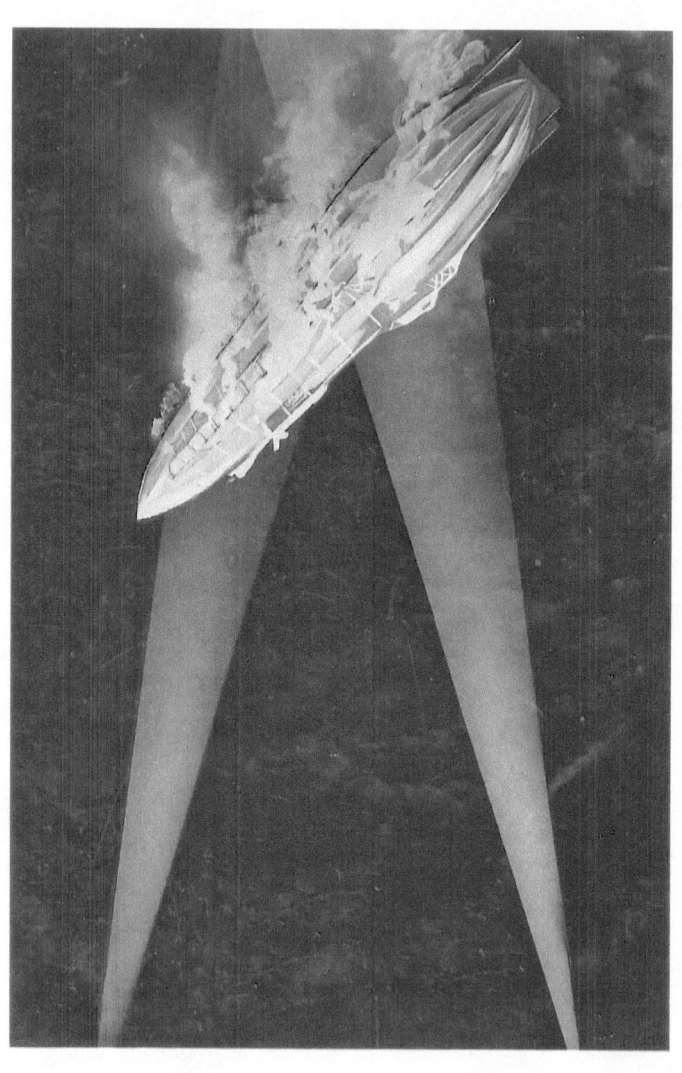

Chapter 1

Zeppelin Nights—September 3, 1916

Baby killers! Violators! Demons of the night!" The woman shouting this abuse is standing in the middle of Charles Street in the heart of London, her hair flying, her mouth open in an ugly scream, her mad eyes bulging and her fist raised, shaking violently at the sky. She's not an escapee from the insane asylum but a well-dressed society woman on her way home from a night at the theatre or a gathering in some upper-class parlour.

It is two thirty in the morning and the only light comes from the half-full moon when it appears through the clouds, the flashes from the anti-aircraft guns and the reflections of the waving searchlights. It's like a scene straight out of hell—guns and bombs crash all around, bright lights explode in the sky and the sharp taste of explosives catches the back of my throat. Hundreds of shadowy figures either rush about madly or, like me, stand immobile, overwhelmed by the spectacle.

Almost directly over me, in the crossed beams of two searchlights, I can make out a cigar-shaped airship pinned like some giant moth to the black heavens above. The lights play along the zeppelin's vast length, and I can see the gondolas hanging below the craft. Inside those gondolas are German airmen, the same men who invaded Belgium two years ago, and who still occupy and ravage my homeland. I am only Manon Wouters, a refugee girl who has become a nurse, but it seems as if my enemies have followed me all the way from Belgium to try to kill me with bombs from the dark sky. I feel like joining the woman in the middle of the road and screaming my fury at them.

"Quite the spectacle, isn't it?" My companion, Major Thomas Owen Macleod, speaks calmly and I'm not sure whether he's referring to the pyrotechnics in the sky or the woman screaming in the road. He's immaculately dressed and the creases in his uniform are still crisp, despite the fact that he's been working in it for almost twenty hours.

"I hate them," I say, my voice rough with emotion. The zeppelin raid has caught us as the major is escorting me back to my flat. We've just finished a late session at Waterloo House, the new headquarters of the British Directorate of Military Intelligence, Section 6, where I am being taught how to create a false new life for myself and not be discovered. I am being taught to become a spy!

"Hate is a strong motivation, Manon," Major Macleod says. Even in the dim light, I can see his brow furrowed in worry. "Hate can make you strong, but in our line of work, it can also kill you. You have to hide every emotion at all times—even the slightest slip can give you away. Can you do that?"

My hate is cold, like ice not fire, but it can still burn. It began when Belgium was invaded and grew as I watched the Germans march arrogantly down the cobbled streets of my hometown in their drab gray uniforms and sinister spiked helmets. But my hatred became complete when they shot the grocer in the town square.

"Do you want to know about my hate, Major? My hometown, Damme, was an important place hundreds of years ago, but now it is a backwater. My father, mother, brother and I lived in a small house by the canal, and my brother and I grew up without a care in the world, playing and riding our bicycles around the flat countryside. When I finished school, I took up nursing. Every day I would cycle half an hour along the canal bank into Bruges to study at the hospital. It was a perfect life, and even after the invasion, I assumed it would continue."

I take a deep breath to steel myself for the next chapter. "The week after the Germans arrived, they claimed that one of their soldiers had been shot at from a window on our street. The shot missed and the soldier was frightened rather than injured, but the Germans were nervous. They took three hostages, including the town grocer. They demanded that whoever had fired the shot come forward for punishment. No one did, and so, on a rainy August morning, the grocer and the two others were executed by firing squad in the town square." I keep my expression emotionless and stare straight into Macleod's eyes. "The grocer was my father."

Macleod does nothing, simply returning my stare. Deep inside, I want him to put his arms around me, comfort me and give me a shoulder to weep on, but I force myself to go on. "I heard the shots from the square, and those sounds changed me forever. They crystallized my hatred into a hard, cold ball that I have nursed inside me ever since."

Macleod nods. "And you ran away after that?"

"I didn't run away," I say calmly. "Mama sold the grocery store and I left home to fight. She begged me to stay, but I was determined. I knew that shooting from windows wouldn't work—the Germans would simply kill more hostages—yet I had to do something. I crossed the border into neutral Holland and found a ship to England. I used my nursing skills in Egypt and France to help young soldiers recover so they could go back to the war and kill Germans for me. Now that I'm being trained as a spy, I finally have a chance to go home and do something direct to help drive the invaders out of my country—and to avenge my father's murder."

A bomb explodes with a dull crump a few blocks away. Macleod says, "We should get on. There are scarcely enough hours for sleep before we begin again tomorrow, and we still have a lot of preparation to do."

We leave the well-dressed woman, still screaming her hate to the sky, and walk west.

"Did you know that this is one of the routes the condemned took to be hanged at Tyburn?" Macleod says. He often comes out with apparently irrelevant pieces of information. He's told me this one before.

"I know," I reply, "it's the origin of your English expression 'going west,' meaning to die."

"We'll make you a fluent English-speaker yet," he laughs.

"Not that it will do me much good in Belgium," I say. "I suspect that my German will be more use."

"You're one of the best agents we've trained, and it won't be long until we send you home. But it's a dangerous game you're getting into. Do you have any doubts?"

We walk in silence for a minute while I consider my answer.

"I'm scared," I admit. "Nursing wounded soldiers was hard work, but it was safe." I think back to the day when Macleod came to the hospital in France and offered me the chance to become a spy. "And there was a young tunneller from Newfoundland, Alec Shorecross, at the hospital where you recruited me. I was—am—very fond of him, and I think he felt the same way about me. In an ideal world, I would go and find Alec, and we would run away to somewhere where there's no war and be happy. But that can't happen. There is a war and we can't run away.

"Of course I have doubts about what I'm about to do. What will my homeland be like? After two years of occupation and war, will I even recognize my mother and brother? But I can't let these thoughts sway me. You are offering me a chance that might make a difference in a cause I believe in. I can't let my fears and the way I feel about Alec stand in the way of that. I only worry that my contribution won't be worth much."

Macleod nods and says gently, "I would be concerned if you didn't have doubts. But be absolutely assured that the work you do will be of vital importance. Trench warfare can't last forever. Next summer or the one after—perhaps sooner if the Americans see sense and join us—we will break through. Then it will be crucial that we have accurate information about the enemy dispositions in Belgium as we advance."

Macleod looks up and gestures to the north, where the searchlights are still playing on the zeppelin as it moves away from the city and out over the countryside. "More immediately, those monsters are coming here from airfields in Belgium, and there is word of new zeppelins that can fly too high for our anti-aircraft guns or fighter planes. The Germans also have huge bombers that could be used against us. We need to know what's going on."

"But you have spies already in Belgium who can tell you that."

"True, but we have very little information on the submarine bases at Bruges, Zeebrugge and Ostend."

"And my brother, Florien, works at the submarine base at Zeebrugge," I say, guessing where Macleod is going with this.

"Exactly. He's uniquely placed to get information to pass on to you, and through the network we'll put you in contact with, you'll be able to pass that information on to us."

"Are the German U-boats as dangerous as those?" I ask, pointing at the departing zeppelin.

"Possibly much more so," Macleod says. "Our naval blockade of Germany is working. People are beginning to starve, and the Germans are just as frustrated as we are that the war has stagnated in the trenches. One way they can change that is to try to starve Britain out of the war."

"Can they do that?"

"With enough U-boats, yes. Britain can't last long if all the ships bringing food are sunk. We would have to make peace or starve. Russia is already showing signs of falling apart, and if we dropped out of the war, France would have to make peace as well. Germany would win."

"But sending the U-boats against unarmed ships is barbaric," I say.

Macleod nods. "It is and it would cause international outrage. It might even force America into the war. America is immensely powerful, but if we starve and Russia collapses and France surrenders while all the American troops and guns are still sitting in New York harbour..." Macleod doesn't need to finish his sentence.

"What can we do?"

"If we can destroy the U-boats before they put to sea, we will save dozens of ships and hundreds—possibly thousands—of lives. And maybe we'll prevent the Germans winning the war. Is that important enough for you?"

"Of course it is," I agree. "I just have to keep remembering that." We've reached the door of my flat. "I'm tired. A few hours sleep and I'll be fine."

"I'll come by and pick you up a bit later," Macleod says. "Let you get an extra hour or two of sleep."

"Thank you."

I'm lifting my key to the lock when the sky brightens to the north. We both look up and see a ball of fire above the buildings. The fire expands into the shape of an elongated cigar that breaks in the middle and slides in slow motion down the dark sky. We both stand transfixed at the beautiful sight. I know men are dying horrifying deaths up there, but I cannot feel pity for them. I hope the screaming woman is watching this too.

"Well," Macleod says, "that's one that won't be back to terrorize us. Good night." He walks off down the street into the darkness.

I stand and watch the zeppelin's fiery end. By sunrise, there will be nothing but twisted girders and charred bodies for the curious to gawk at. I unlock the door, go quietly up the stairs and collapse onto my bed.

Despite my tiredness, sleep won't come. I will go back to Belgium with my real identity—Manon Wouters, a trainee nurse from the town of Damme, near Bruges. What will change is the story of my life over the past two years. Instead of nursing Allied soldiers back to health, I will have been working on a farm in eastern Belgium for a distant relative. Of course, the relative who can confirm this is a resistance worker for an organization called La Dame Blanche. I have seen photographs of this woman and the farm, and I have learned about this false life that has been created for me. I have returned to Damme, I will say, because I miss my mother and my younger brother.

It will work if nobody looks too closely, and why should they? As Macleod continually tells me, "The most convincing lies are based on truth," and most of my life is true. Once I am back in Damme, I will return to work at the hospital in Bruges, which will give me the opportunity to collect information from wounded German soldiers and sailors. Macleod also says, "Wounded soldiers often fall in love with their nurses. They tell them things they shouldn't."

I think of Alec Shorecross. He fell in love with me—the difference is that I think I fell in love with Alec too. I pray that he is surviving the madness that is overwhelming this world. I wish I had said goodbye to him properly, but I couldn't. I'm sure Alec was on the verge of telling me he loved me when we were interrupted. If I had gone back to talk to him after Macleod made the offer to train me as a spy, he would have said it and I would never have had the strength to leave the hospital and do what I am about to.

Thoughts of Alec comfort me and ease the turmoil of my mind. As I drift off to sleep, I promise myself that I will write to him before I leave for Belgium. I don't wake up until one of my flatmates bangs on my door to tell me that Macleod is waiting downstairs to take me off to another day of training.

Chapter 2

Fear of Flying—December 8, 1916

I am more terrified than I have ever been. My training has been thorough and detailed: I know the false pieces of my life so well that I dream about them. I have my identity papers, I'm wearing clothes made in Belgium, and I've polished my German until it is flawless. There's just one thing Major Macleod forgot—he never sent me up in an airplane.

I knew perfectly well that to begin my work, I would be flown over the trenches and landed in a field near Damme, but I was focused on more immediate issues and assumed it would be no problem. As time passed, I found myself watching planes overhead and thinking how fragile they looked, but I still looked upon my flight as just something unpleasant that had to be done. Now I'm in a field in France, sitting in the open cockpit of what my pilot calls an F.E.2b, and even though we haven't yet left the ground, I think I'm going to throw up.

This thing can't possibly fly. I'm wrapped in a thick sheepskin jacket, with a leather helmet and goggles on my head, and crouched in a horribly exposed cockpit. If I had the courage, I could lean forward and look straight down to the ground. The pilot, a cheerful young Englishman, sits behind and slightly above me. Behind him is a huge, thundering engine and the massive two-bladed propeller that will push us forward. Farther back, several fragile struts support a tiny tail, and on either side, impossibly flimsy wings stretch out into the silvery moonlight. I swallow convulsively, desperate to keep the contents of my stomach in place.

"It's called a pusher," the pilot informs me cheerfully, leaning forward to shout in my ear. "Propeller's at the back, you see, pushing us forward. That allows the observer—the chap who sits where you are—a clear field of fire without having to shoot through the propeller. We decided it was best not to give you a Lewis gun. Don't want any accidents, what?"

I grunt through clenched teeth, praying that he will shut up and let me suffer in peace. He doesn't.

"These tubs were a godsend last year, when the Fokkers were at their worst. A bit slow now, but still maneuverable. One of these brought down Immelmann this past summer. It'll do until something better comes along, and it's good for night work like this and the odd bombing mission."

I have no idea what he's talking about and I don't care. I just want my fear to end.

"Right-ho, then. Shall we take off?"

I lean forward and throw up on the cockpit floor, trying to avoid the battered suitcase at my feet. If my cheerful pilot notices, he's too polite to mention it.

The engine note changes and we begin to move forward, bumping over the field. The ground seems to rush past me at an insane speed. I throw up again. As I sit back up, I gradually become aware that the bumping has stopped. Cold wind rushes past my cheeks. We're airborne. I feel a slight thrill. Then I make the mistake of looking over the side. In the moonlight, dark shapes rush by below us. Before dizziness overwhelms me, I can make out a few derelict buildings, a battery of heavy artillery and the straight line of a country road. I slump back as low as I can and grip the edges of the cockpit, glad that there's nothing left in my stomach to come up.

"We'll fly low and fast over the front line," the pilot shouts at me. "That will give us the best chance of avoiding the anti-aircraft guns."

I don't like his use of the word chance, but I try to focus and push my fear down. Hiding my fear is something I'll have to do, like pushing my hatred down so it won't show. I concentrate on my breathing, paying attention to every breath in through my nose and every breath out through my mouth. Fear tries to push its way into my thoughts, but I push back and focus my awareness on my next breath—in, out, in, out...

I feel my hands relax on the cockpit edge and force myself to sit upright. I look up at the sky. We're flying east, away from where the sun set two hours ago. The moon is high in the sky and almost full. Wispy clouds drift across it like torn pieces of curtain. I try to pick out familiar constellations, but the clouds are too thick and the moon too bright to allow more than an occasional glimpse of the brightest stars.

Studying the familiar sky helps me relax more and I risk lowering my eyes. Ahead, occasional bright orange flashes light up the horizon. I assume they must be German guns near the front lines. It's strangely beautiful, a weird moving picture show in magical colour with the music drowned out by the plane's thudding engine. I remember as a child watching a thunderstorm and trying to predict where the next lightning flash would occur. I do the same here, but the flashes are random and I only ever manage to see them at the edges of my vision.

Over to my left, a bright pinpoint of light soars up in a long, lazy arc. At its highest point, it hangs for a moment before bursting into an incredibly bright white fireball that drifts down to the ground. Entranced, I forget my fear and lean over to look down. Below me, I see a bewildering complexity of ghostly white marks zigzagging across the landscape—the front lines. I know that thousands of men are down there trying to kill one another, but the terrain below me is empty. It's a dead landscape. All signs of life—farms, villages, fields, roads, livestock—have vanished. All that remains are shell holes, the water in them gleaming like mercury in the light. The flare fades into darkness, then the red burst of an exploding shell shocks me out of my reverie and I slump back in my seat.

"Poor blighters," the pilot says. "Rather be up here than down there any day."

The next time I look over the edge, the war has vanished. We're over open countryside. Undamaged poplar trees line the roads. Over to my right, a train puffs sedately on its way. To my left, the lights of a small village twinkle calmly. It looks as if I am over the only place in the world not ravaged by war, but it's an illusion. Down there is Belgium, my homeland, and the invaders who have ruled her ruthlessly for more than two years.

"Almost there now," the pilot shouts. "Our field is just beyond that clump of trees. I hope the farmer hasn't plowed it since we last checked."

I watch as the trees approach and sweep under us, the tops a few feet below our wheels. Once past the trees, we drop sickeningly and bump and rumble across the pasture.

"Out you pop now," the pilot says cheerily as soon as we come to a halt. "If you go north along that road ahead of us, you should be in Damme in a couple of hours."

I clamber clumsily out of the cockpit, dragging my suitcase after me. My knees are so weak I can barely stand, but I'm glad to be alive and back on solid ground.

"Thank you," I say.

"My pleasure, but you probably don't want to found wandering around Belgium in a Royal Flying Corps sheepskin jacket, helmet and goggles."

"Of course." I laugh nervously, pull off the goggles, helmet and jacket, and stuff them back in the cockpit. "Thank you again."

"Good luck."

I stand in the shadows of the trees and watch as the plane bumps its way over the field and—almost reluctantly, it seems—hauls itself into the air. The wings waggle in farewell as it banks over me and heads west, back to friendly territory. I wait until the last rumble of its engine dies away and a blanket of silence descends over me. I continue to stand with my back against a tree, savouring the quiet.

London was never silent. There were always people about, and their chatter was set against a background of clopping horses, rattling cart wheels and the clank of motor cars, taxicabs and buses moving along the cobbled streets. I don't think my surroundings have been this calm since the war began.

As my ears adjust, I begin to hear other sounds—the rustle of a small animal in the underbrush, and the cry of a hunted creature nearby. Beneath the natural sounds, there's something else, barely there at the limits of awareness. It takes me a moment to understand that I'm listening to the sounds of war, the heavy guns far to the west. This makes me realize that I have work to do, and that I'm probably in more danger than the soldier huddled in his muddy trench beneath the guns.

I brush leaves off my coat, hoist my battered suitcase and step out onto the road. It's deserted in both directions as far as I can see in the moonlight. Keeping close to the trees, I set off toward Damme.

My pilot's estimate of two hours of walking was optimistic. It must be closer to four, and it feels even longer to my feet in their unsuitable shoes and my arms aching from carrying my suitcase. Three times I've taken refuge in the roadside ditch when I've heard horses approach, but no one has noticed me.

I move slowly from shadow to shadow through the outskirts of Damme, but no one is around at this time of night. Even by moonlight, everything is hauntingly familiar—the cobbled

Kerkstraat, the neat rows of gabled houses, the squat tower of the church standing sentinel over the town. I skirt the town square where I have both happy memories of playing as a child and dark ones of father's execution.

I turn up Slekstraat, and suddenly I'm standing at the door of my house. I can hardly breathe because the emotion of the moment is so tight in my chest. I lift the door knocker and let it fall. It seems forever until I hear shuffling footsteps from inside. The latch is lifted and my mother is standing there.

"Mama," I say softly.

"Manon, is it you?"

"Yes."

Suddenly I am enveloped in my mother's tearful embrace and pulled inside. I have come home.

Chapter 3

Home—December 9, 1916

After seemingly endless tears and hugs, Mama sits me down at the kitchen table and, despite the fact that it is well past midnight, insists on feeding me.

"The Germans take the best of everything," she says as she clatters the pots and pans. "Soon it will be impossible to get anything that we don't grow ourselves. We will be living on turnips and potatoes."

I sit in silence, letting Mama chatter on while I luxuriate in my surroundings. Everything around me is familiar—the smells wafting from the soup pot on the stove, the cast-iron skillets hanging from the hooks above the fireplace, the rough feel of the thick wooden table where I spent much of my childhood puzzling over homework. I let my finger trace out the initials that Florien and I dug into the tabletop one day many years ago. Papa was very cross with us, but he never sanded the table to get rid of our marks.

"It's only vegetable soup," Mama says, placing a steaming bowl before me. "But it is hearty. It will build up your strength better than the foreign food you must have been forced to eat for so long."

"Foreign food was all right, Mama," I say as I take the first mouthful. "Not as good as your cooking, though, and some of the dishes in Egypt were a bit strange."

"Egypt, my heavens! You did get around," Mama says as she sits opposite me at the table. "Two years you've been away," she adds wistfully. "You look much older. A real woman now. My little girl's gone."

"Did you not get any of my letters?" I ask. "I received two of yours and sent you several."

"No, dear. None arrived. I was able to get a couple out because there was a nice Red Cross man staying in town. He was Danish, I think. Now that you're home, you must tell me every detail of where you were and what you did."

Between mouthfuls of soup, I tell Mama about nursing the soldiers in Egypt and France. I tell her I was in London, but I say I was a nurse there as well. I don't want her to know that I am here as a spy.

"If anyone asks where I've been," I say, telling Mama what I agreed with Macleod, "you must tell them that I went to stay with relatives in the east. It wouldn't be good for the Germans to discover that I left the country to nurse their enemies."

"Of course." Mama's brow furrows in worry. "Things are not good here, and they will not get better. Some people say that the war will never end, and that we will be a part of Germany forever. You escaped all this. Why did you come back?"

"I thought I should use my skills as a nurse to help my own people. Tomorrow I will go to Bruges and get my old job back."

"You won't be helping many of your own people. Most of the beds now are filled with German soldiers and sailors. Is that what you want?"

In truth, that is what I want. It's the German soldiers and sailors who will give me information that I can pass on. But I can't tell Mama that. To avoid answering, I make a joke.

"You see through me too easily, Mama. The real reason I returned was because I missed your turnip and potato soup."

Mama laughs and reaches for my hand across the table.

"I really did miss you and Florien terribly," I say.

At the mention of my brother, Mama's expression darkens. "You'll find your brother much changed."

"In what way?"

"You remember how happy-go-lucky he always was?"

"Of course. He never seemed to have a care in the world."

"Now you would swear he carries the entire world on his shoulders. I don't think you will know him. The war has destroyed the Florien you once knew. He gets out of bed each morning and barely grunts hello to me. The truck collects him and the other workers and takes them to Zeebrugge. He comes home late, if he comes home at all, and goes straight to bed. I hardly see him, let alone talk with him. I try to get him to eat supper, but he always says he ate at work. And he drinks too much. Every night he's out with a real rough crowd. I get so worried."

"It must be hard for Florien, being forced to work for the men who killed Papa," I say in my brother's defence.

"That's not it." Mama twists the dishtowel between her work-reddened hands. "Florien never talks about his father. It's as if he never existed. I gave your brother Papa's pocket watch. I thought it would be something to remind him. Do you know what he did?"

I shake my head.

"He sold it. When I questioned him about it, he said he had done it to buy food. But he didn't buy food—he bought alcohol for himself and his cronies."

I'm shocked at what Mama's telling me. None of this sounds like the sweet, sensitive brother I used to know.

"But that's not the worst thing," Mama goes on. "He admires the Germans."

I stare at her in horror. "That can't be right. You must be mistaken."

Mama gazes at me sadly, suddenly looking much older than I remember. "There's no mistake," she says. "Soon after you escaped, Florien joined the Flemish Movement."

"What is the Flemish Movement?"

"They want to split Belgium in two—a Flemish/Dutch half and a Walloon/French half. We have always been a country of two cultures, but we have managed. Now the Germans think it would be easier to govern a split country, so they support the Flemish Movement."

"So Florien likes the Germans because he thinks they will create a Flemish country? But it makes no sense! He was never political."

"That has changed. On the rare occasions that I can get him to talk to me, all he can say is that we need to be a separate country and Germany will help us achieve that. He idolizes the Germans. He praises how well organized they are and how wonderful their submarines and guns are. I'm at my wits end. I don't know what I can do with him anymore. Perhaps your return will make him see things differently. Will you try talking to him?"

"Of course, Mama." But I have no idea what I'll say. I had planned on talking to Florien—but to persuade him to spy for Britain. The fact that he is pro-German is a shock and will make my task much more difficult. Why has he changed so much?

My thoughts are interrupted by the front door opening noisily. Florien, swaying slightly, stands in the kitchen doorway, staring at me.

"What are you doing here?" he asks.

"Is that any way to welcome your sister home, little brother?" I stand up and step toward him. "I came back to see you and Mama."

"After you deserted us for two years?" Florien almost spits the words out. "You abandon Mama and me to go off and live the high life."

"Hardly the high life," I say. "I was a nurse in Egypt, France and London."

"That's very noble." Florien's voice is dripping with sarcasm. "No doubt you were nursing those stupid British soldiers. They shouldn't even be here. It's not their war."

I decide not to argue with him. "Well, I'm home now, and I was hoping for a welcoming hug."

Florien looks uncertain for a moment, but then his expression hardens. "How did you get back here?"

I can hardly tell him that I was brought in by a British plane. "The same way I got out," I say as calmly as possible. "Through the border with Holland."

"But that's impossible. The Germans have built a wire fence all along the border. There are two thousand volts running through it. Anyone who touches the wire dies."

"There are ways," I say, thankful that Macleod had prepared me for this as well. "Some communities are cut in half by the wire. The Germans let people through on market days. I just had to persuade a farmer to take me through on his apple cart."

"I suppose you think you're very clever," Florien says.

"I don't, but I am sorry that you don't seem pleased to see your big sister."

I step forward again and open my arms for a hug, but Florien is too wrapped up in his anger.

"You should have stayed on the other side of the wire," he snarls. Then he turns on his heel and clumps along the corridor to his room.

Overwhelmed by sadness, I sit back down at the table.

"You see what he is like," Mama says. "Things are difficult, but we could get through if we stuck together as a family. I don't know how long I can stand him being like this."

"Everything will be fine," I say. "When Florien's calmed down tomorrow, I'll talk to him. He'll come around. Everything will be good now that I'm home."

To comfort Mama, I force as much conviction as I can into my voice, but it must be obvious that I don't believe a word I'm saying. I left Belgium because I had lost my father. Now I'm back and I seem to have lost my brother as well.

Chapter 4

Contact—December 9, 1916

The watery sun is low on the horizon and offers little warmth, but it's still good to see. I'm cycling along the towpath beside the canal that leads to Bruges, and it's so quiet and peaceful that I can almost imagine there's no war on. My mind drifts back to the carefree days when I used to cycle this path, excited to be heading for the hospital and my nursing training. Some days Florien would cycle with me, just for the fun of it. We would race short stretches and I would always let him win.

Thoughts of Florien bring my mood down. I am shocked by his attitude. How could he have changed so much? Despite his late arrival last night, he was gone by the time I got out of bed. I was relieved that I didn't have to face him again, but that just made me feel guilty.

Mama cooked me two precious eggs for breakfast and I set off for the location I had been given in Bruges for my contact in La Dame Blanche. The coded conversation we will use to recognize each other runs through my head. I am to go to the market square and sit on the steps of the statue to the great Flemish heroes Jan Breydel and Pieter de Coninck. My contact will approach me and say, "Do you think we'll have a white Christmas this year?" I am to reply, "I think it will be many years until we have a white Christmas." After that, despite all my training, I really have no idea what to expect.

"Halt!"

A policeman steps in front of me as I enter the outskirts of Bruges. I brake to a stop just inches from him. He's a regular Belgian policeman and not much older than me. He's frowning at me, but his brown eyes don't look threatening.

"Papers," he demands.

I hand over my identity papers.

"Manon Wouters," he says as he scans the documents. "Where are you coming from?"

"My home in Damme," I reply.

"And why are you coming to Bruges?"

"I'm a nurse. I'm coming to begin work in the hospital."

"Coming to begin work?" He stares hard at me and I have to struggle to quell the butterflies that are suddenly active in my stomach. "You are a nurse who lives in Damme and you have not already been working in the hospital?"

I realize my mistake. I shouldn't have said I was beginning work.

"I worked here before," I say with what I hope is a disarming smile. "I did my training in Bruges, but when the war broke out, Mama thought I should go and stay with a relative in the country. I have only just returned from there."

He nods and I hope I have passed the test, but he has one more question. "Why did you come back?"

I let out a small laugh that I hope is convincing. "I was bored in the country. The most exciting thing to do was milk the cows. And being woken every morning at daybreak by the cockerels is wearing after a while."

I broaden my smile, but the policeman doesn't return it. He does, however, give me my papers back.

"Welcome back," he says. "But after a few weeks of city food, I think you'll miss the cockerels and the fresh milk."

I cycle on, pleased that I have passed my first test as a spy. As ordered, I park my bicycle in the market square and sit on the steps at the base of the statue. Even in the sun, everything looks gray. There are not many people around—it's early and there's little to buy in the shops—but those who are in the square shuffle around aimlessly, nodding at those they pass. There are no clusters of people discussing local affairs or gossiping about neighbours, no gangs of children shouting gleefully as they chase hoops or play ball games. A few buildings around the square have made an attempt at putting up festive decorations, but that only emphasizes the drabness of everything else.

Two bored-looking German soldiers stand on either side of the arch beneath the belfry tower, making me wonder if this is such a good location for a couple of spies to meet. I watch the soldiers out of the corner of my eye, but they don't seem interested in anything going on in the square.

A German officer strides across the square. He passes within a few feet of me, but doesn't even glance in my direction. The two soldiers stand straight and salute as he passes, then slump back into their previous indifference.

As I watch the people pass across the square, I try to guess who might be a member of La Dame Blanche. I spot a couple of candidates—an old woman who wanders back and forth several times, and a younger woman who glances over at me four times—but both leave without asking me about Christmas.

I wonder what I'll do if no one shows up. Already, I think I've been here too long. If I stay much longer, even the bored soldiers will begin to notice me. Should I go to the hospital and ask about work? Should I head home? Has something gone wrong?

"Manon Wouters, I thought you said you were going to the hospital." I jerk upright and turn to see the young policemen who stopped me earlier. He looks very serious and I feel his eyes drilling into me. "Yet here I find you, sitting by a statue in the square."

"I...I felt tired. I needed to sit." I stumble over my words. Out of the corner of my eye, I see the German guards looking over at us. Is the policeman going to summon them? Am I to be arrested before I even begin my life as a spy? "I didn't sleep much last night."

"And why was that?" he says, interrogating me.

I remember Major Macleod telling me, "The best lies are the ones that stick closest to the truth."

"I arrived home late," I explain. "Remember I told you that I came from my relative's farm in the east? It was a long walk, and very few people offer lifts to travellers these days. My mama wanted to hear all my news, so I had only an hour or two of sleep. I thought I would rest here for a few minutes before going to the hospital. I must have dozed off."

The policeman looks long at me, as if judging my story. "I think you had better come along with me," he says at last.

My heart is racing and I'm frantically trying to think of something to say when he adds, "But first, I have another question for you: Do you think we'll have a white Christmas this year?"

It takes me a moment to realize what he has said. Eventually, I manage to stammer, "I think it will be many years until we have a white Christmas."

The policeman nods. "And now we should go, before we attract any more attention."

I look over and see that the soldiers are both staring in our direction.

"Excuse me," the policeman says as he grabs my arm firmly with his left hand. With his right, he grasps the handlebars of my bicycle and leads me across the square. I see one soldier lean towards his companion and say something. Both of them laugh.

"It is easier to talk while we walk," the policeman says. "Fewer people can overhear. You did well with your story, but you made a mistake saying you were just beginning work at the hospital."

I have trouble replying. Even though I know this is my contact, my mouth is dry with fear. Will all spying be like this? Am I facing a life of constant confusion and terror?

"I know. It won't happen again," I reply, swallowing hard. "What's your name?"

"We don't deal much in names, but you can call me Pieter."

We walk in silence for a while. Pieter has let go of my arm and we walk side by side like any young couple out for a stroll.

"I thought that La Dame Blanche was a network run by women," I say.

Pieter glances around. "It's best not to use that term," he says quietly, "but you are correct—it is mostly a group of women. However, there are organizations where it's useful for us to have members that do not allow women to join."

"Organizations such as the police?" I suggest.

Pieter nods, and for the first time I see him smile, but it soon fades.

"We don't have much time, so I must speak fast. Your main task will be to obtain information from the German sailors and soldiers being treated in the hospital."

"But I don't even have my job there back yet," I say.

"That's all taken care of," Pieter explains. "You'll be starting your first shift today. You must collect every piece of information you can, even the most trivial. Even details like what unit a soldier is in and where and when he was wounded tell us what regiment was in the German front lines at a specific place and time. We also want you to pay particular attention to any German sailors or workers from the docks here in Bruges, in Zeebrugge or in Ostend. Every tiny piece of information, however insignificant, is a part of the larger jigsaw puzzle that will help us win this war and free our country."

"How do I get the information to you?"

"You don't. I live in Maldegem and rarely come into town. A go-between will collect the information you gather and pass it on to me. I have contacts who will make sure the information reaches the people who can make the best use of it."

I wonder if one of the people who can make the best use of my information is Major Macleod in London. I find it comforting that there might be a line of contacts stretching from me in the hospital in Bruges to Macleod in military intelligence in London. I feel less alone.

"Who will my contact be?" I ask.

"You won't know. We try to keep each link in the chain as separate as possible. That way, if someone is captured he or she cannot betray others in the network. You will write down whatever you find out on a small piece of paper. Every day you will place that paper behind the cistern in the second cubicle from the end in the nurses' washroom beside the cafeteria."

"What if I need to contact someone," I ask.

"In that case, leave a piece of paper with the words Jan Breydel written on it behind the cistern and be at the statue first thing the following morning. If we need to contact you, you will find a note with Pieter de Coninck written on it. That will tell you to be at the statue the following morning."

I nod. It sounds straightforward, if not very exciting. But then, I'm not sure excitement's what I want.

"You will do well," Pieter says. He hands me my bicycle and I look up to see that we are at the hospital. "Pick up what information you can, but keep a low profile and stay out of trouble."

"Thank you, Pieter," I say and head for the hospital doors.

"Be careful," he says to my retreating back.

At the doors, I lean my bicycle against the wall and look back, but Pieter has disappeared.

Chapter 5

Settling In—February 1917

I am welcomed with open arms at the hospital. The wards are so overcrowded and the nurses so overworked that they need any help they can get. In fact, I'm rushed off my feet my first day and don't get home until late.

At first I have trouble pretending to be friendly with the soldiers. After all, if I help them get well, they'll go back to the front and perhaps kill the young British soldiers I cared for in France. However, going back to work reminds me of my time in France, and of nursing Alec back to health. I begin to see the patients in Bruges less as the enemy and more as scared, injured boys no different from the ones on the other side of the trenches. I find it easier to be kind to them, and they respond by talking more easily to me.

Of course, all they want to talk about is home and family, and how much they are looking forward to having some leave when they're released from the hospital. I have to listen to everything to pick up the occasional useful nugget of information, because I can't raise suspicion by showing too much interest in details such as where they served and what their regiment is. I write down everything that seems important and place my notes behind the cistern. I'm tempted to try to find out who my contact is, and I sometimes sit in the cafeteria watching the door to the toilet. But I can see no pattern to the movement of people in and out.

As the days and then the weeks drag past, boredom begins to take a toll. Is the information I'm passing on really worth anything? I begin to feel useless and wonder if I have made the right choice in coming home. The work at the hospital keeps me busy, but I need to feel that I am doing something important.

As the cold and hungry winter drags on, my mood sinks lower. The only bright spot is my friendship with Amelie, a fellow nurse who also lives in Damme. When we have the same shifts, we cycle in together and talk about the war, our families and our work. She's the same age as me and I vaguely remember her from school, but we weren't close. Now, thrown together in the frantic chaos of the hospital, we discover that we have much in common. She too lives with her mother, although her father, unlike mine, is still alive and working in a factory somewhere in Germany. We don't talk about anything very serious. We discuss the meals we'll eat when the war is over, and I tell her all about Alec and how I feel about him.

However miserable I am, a conversation with Amelie usually raises my spirits, but I always have feelings of guilt and loneliness when we talk. I am a spy and can never drop my guard. I have secrets that I can't tell to anyone. Amelie is my closest friend in Bruges, but I can never fully trust her. One slip, one wrong word, one confidence innocently repeated to the wrong person can mean prison—or worse. Macleod never told me how lonely the life of a spy would be.

At least my return has helped Mama. She has become more cheerful and less worried about Florien. My small salary from the hospital helps as well, and we can afford little luxuries, even at the exorbitant prices of the black market. We manage to get hold of a whole goose for Christmas dinner. That day is almost like old times and Florien is on his best behaviour.

I see very little of Florien, but when I do, he is often sullen and cold. Between his work at the U-boat base and his evenings drinking with his cronies, he's not home much. I try a couple of times to talk to him about the war, but all he does is spout nonsense about how powerful the Germans are and how wonderful everything will be when they give us a separate Flemish state.

In January, Florien is transferred from Zeebrugge to the docks in Bruges, where a lot of construction is going on. I pass on the news of Florien's move to London and get an urgent reply to try to recruit him and find out what work is being done there. I delay doing anything, though, because I think it's pointless to approach my brother and I want to avoid a fight with him.

In my free time, I take bicycle trips to the canal that runs from Bruges to Zeebrugge. A great deal of German navy traffic passes along this canal, but it is heavily patrolled and there are only a few places where it is possible to watch the water. I count a varied collection of craft, from fast torpedo boats to heavily armed destroyers, but the U-boats come and go at night. I have a special permit to be out during the dusk-to-dawn curfew because of the shifts I work at the hospital, but it only applies to the route from Damme to Bruges and it would be suspicious if I was discovered cycling around the countryside near military installations.

At the beginning of February, real winter arrives with a vengeance. The temperature plummets, the canals freeze and the ground vanishes beneath inches of snow. People shuffle along the streets, bundled in every piece of clothing they own. Many have bales of sticks tied to their backs so they can feed the stove in their kitchen and keep at least one room of their house warm. At the hospital we begin to see dockyard workers with frostbitten fingers and toes.

If it is particularly cold or snowing heavily, Amelie and I sleep at the hospital, huddled for warmth in the basement boiler room. That's where we are early on the morning of February 3, when Bruges is bombed for the first time.

"Listen." Amelie shakes me awake.

At first I can hear only a dull thumping—more a vibration through the ground than a sound. "What is it?"

Amelie shrugs. We pull on our coats and head out to the hospital courtyard. The cold is frightful, but a number of other people are standing around, staring at the spectacle over the dockyards on the northern edge of the city.

Powerful searchlight beams crisscross the black sky, forming cones where they intersect in their hunt for the attackers. Anti-aircraft shells explode in grey puffs of smoke and lines of startlingly green flares rise in the sky like great jade necklaces. Tiny aircraft flash in and out of the searchlight beams and dodge between the flares like dragonflies. The bombs they drop explode in a burst of red below. The crash of explosions and the distant grumble of the aircraft engines accompany this dramatic, deadly fireworks display.

Suddenly, the planes are gone. The searchlights and explosions follow them for a while, but then they cease as well. Peace returns to the night.

Amelie and I return inside to the cafeteria. "I never thought that they would bomb us here," I say, wrapping my cold hands around a mug of a warm drink that's called coffee but tastes nothing like it. "I hope Florien's all right."

"I hope so too," Amelie says. "But it wasn't a large raid. I counted only five or six airplanes, and not many bombs were dropped. Most of the spectacle was from the searchlights and the anti-aircraft guns. I hope none of the bombs landed on the town."

Amelie's hope is misplaced. One of the bombs landed on a house near the docks and the explosion wounded a ten-year-old boy. He arrives at the hospital soon after we begin our shift. The boy's wound isn't bad—a bomb fragment has cut his leg—but the sight of a wounded child reminds me of the bombing I witnessed in London. The difference is that this child has been injured by a friendly bomb. I think back to the woman screaming in the street the night of the zeppelin raid. Would she scream her anger at the British planes if she could see this wounded boy? Why is everything becoming so complicated?

~~~~~

There are other raids as the cold weather of February continues. They are larger and some are in daylight. The number of injured civilians we see at the hospital increases. People walk the streets grim-faced, their brows etched with worry about relatives in German work camps and the daily grind of finding enough food and fuel. It's a dark winter. The only bright spot is when America severs diplomatic relations with Germany. It's a step toward declaring war, but will it be too late? The German newspapers trumpet the dramatic increase in the number of ships being sunk by U-boats and how close Britain is to starving. I feel helpless.

One day in March, I find Florien at the kitchen table hunched over a large sheet of paper.

"What are you working on?" I ask, still eager to find a point of connection between us, and feeling guilty that I have made no attempt to recruit him despite several orders from Major Macleod. He is desperate for information on the building going on at the Bruges docks.

Florien stands up. "I'm charting the tonnages of British merchant ships sunk," he says proudly. "See? In January, we sunk more than three hundred thousand tons of shipping. February was a record month—over five hundred thousand tons—and March looks as if we might top six hundred thousand tons. The British can't last long at this rate."

I bite back my anger and try to appeal to Florien's humanity. "Every one of those ships is filled with sailors, and they are given no warning when a submarine attacks."

"That's not true," Florien says. He's strangely happy and keen to explain things to me. "British propaganda paints the submariners as devils, but really they are heroes. When a U-boat finds a merchant ship, it surfaces and orders the crew to take to the lifeboats before sinking the vessel."

"I've heard that's not always the case," I say calmly.

"Perhaps not," Florien says, "but that is the fault of the British. They use decoy ships. When a U-boat surfaces, panels in the side of a harmless-looking merchantman drop, revealing hidden guns. Can you blame a U-boat captain for not risking his vessel and his crew?"

I try a different approach. "Do the Germans have enough U-boats to keep this up long enough to starve Britain?"

"No problem," Florien says. "There are twenty-five U-boats based in Bruges alone, and more at Zeebrugge and Ostend. Only five have been lost, and they've been replaced." He leans closer to me and says confidentially, "There is talk of converting the large transport U-boats into ocean-going hunters. They could carry many more torpedoes and even sink ships in New York harbour if the Americans are stupid enough to join this war."

"New York!" I exclaim, horrified at the thought of U-boats being able to range so far.

Florien mistakes my reaction for admiration. "Incredible, isn't it?" he says. "Of course, the really big U-boats won't fit in Bruges. They'll have to sail from Ostend or Kiel."

I can't believe Florien is giving away so much information. I make mental notes of everything he tells me and try to keep him talking.

"I worry about you working at the docks with all the bombing going on. I don't want to see you carried into the hospital one day."

"I'll be fine," he says with a smile. He can't stop himself from boasting about how clever the invaders are. "The Germans have raised a thick reinforced concrete roof over much of the area where I work. Only a direct hit from a very large bomb would damage it. And if the bombing gets too heavy, we can take refuge in the pens we are building for the U-boats—they have roofs several feet thick.

Nothing can destroy them." He bends and rolls up his paper. "I must go and pin this on my wall. One day it will be an accurate chart of Britain's defeat."

I stand and watch my brother's retreating back. He's happier than I have seen him since my return. It was like talking to the old Florien—except for the subject of our conversation. I feel glad that we seem to have reconnected but guilty that I will have to pass on everything we talked about. Betraying one's own family—just another aspect of the life of a spy. Frowning, I head for my room to write down all that Florien said.

Chapter 6

A New Threat—April 6, 1917

As winter turns to spring, I continue to place scraps of paper with the information I have collected behind the cistern in the washroom at the hospital. I rarely get any feedback or instructions in return. It's odd that work so monotonous can be so dangerous, and I have to keep reminding myself that I'm running a serious risk whenever I place a message.

Ever since my conversation with Florien, my brother has withdrawn back into himself, despite my trying to re-engage him several times. He's working longer hours, and instead of coming home to rest when he's done, he disappears almost every night to drink with his gang of friends. I'll just have to be patient. At least, I have received no more requests to recruit him. Perhaps Major Macleod assumes that I've already persuaded him to work for us.

One Thursday, I find a slip of paper behind the cistern. I pull it out and read, "Pieter de Coninck." It's the code telling me to be at the statue in the market square first thing the next morning. My heart thumps with excited anticipation. Am I to be given an important task? What will it be? Will it be dangerous?

The next morning, I'm up early and cycling along the canal as the sun hauls itself above the horizon. I splash through puddles left by the overnight rain, staining my boots and skirt with mud, but I don't mind. I feel like a small child on Christmas morning.

I have to force myself to slow down so as not to arrive at the market square too early. I stroll across the empty space as casually as possible, worried that the German soldiers posted there can see my excitement and hear my heartbeat. I am oddly eager to see Pieter again, and as I take my place below the statue, I look around the square trying to spot him. But the only familiar face I see is Amelie pushing her bicycle toward the hospital. I look away, but she spots me and waves. She swings her bicycle round and joins me on the steps.

"Hello, Manon," she says cheerfully as she sits down. "You stopped to take the air on the way to work?"

"I'm feeling a bit tired," I say, "so I stopped for a rest. Don't let me hold you up. I'll follow along shortly."

"I'm in no hurry. We're so busy, it's important to remember to take these small moments to rest."

Now I'm worried. When Pieter sees me with Amelie, he won't come and give me my assignment. What will I do then? Come back tomorrow?

I'm trying to think of a way to get rid of Amelie when she leans closer and murmurs, "I missed not having a white Christmas last year. As you said, it will be a long time until we have another one."

I turn and stare at my friend.

She smiles and goes on, "I think I've had enough of a rest. Let's walk to work. We can go down by the canal."

"Okay," I stammer, stunned to discover that Amelie is part of La Dame Blanche. Pushing our bicycles, we set off out of the square. "I was expecting Pieter."

"It will be more natural for you and I to be seen together," Amelie says. She's smiling as we talk and anyone watching would think we're gossiping or discussing boyfriends.

"Are you the one who picks up my information?"

"Yes. I'm the first link in the chain. There were many times that I wanted to tell you, but we must be careful."

I laugh out loud. "All winter, I've agonized that I might let something slip when I'm talking to you, and you're the one person I could have talked to! I've looked at everyone in the hospital, wondering who was taking my pieces of paper from behind the cistern, and all the while, you were sitting right beside me."

Amelie's smile broadens. "You did well. You never gave anything away. And your information is good, by the way. Very thorough."

"And useful?" I ask.

"Of course. I know it's sometimes difficult to see how what we do fits into the larger picture, but trust me it does. London was particularly pleased with the information about the U-boat pens at the dockyard here in Bruges."

"Thank you," I say. "So are you revealing your identity to me now because you have a job for me?"

"Do you think you're ready?"

"More than ready. Do you want me to find out more about the U-boats?" I ask, wondering how I can possibly do that.

"Eventually, yes, but something else has come up. You're no doubt aware of the zeppelin raids on England?"

"All too aware," I say.

"Many of the zeppelins fly from airfields in Belgium."

"I know that too," I say. "And I was told that the Germans are developing a new one that can fly above the defences."

"That is true," Amelie says, "but they're not important. zeppelins are a good propaganda weapon, but winds can blow them off course too easily and most raiders never reach their target, dropping their bombs in the sea or on open fields. The new zeppelins can fly higher but they carry fewer bombs, and navigation will be even more difficult from such a height. They will scare the civilians, but the real danger comes from the new German bombers."

"I was told something in London about large bombers."

"Yes, the Germans have these planes called Gothas. They have an enormous wingspan and can carry half a ton of bombs. The bombs that the British drop on the docks here are only a tenth that size."

As I struggle to imagine the devastation these Gothas could do, Amelie goes on. "The Germans have used Gotha bombers in the east and over France for some time, but—" She breaks off as a pair of workmen walk past us in the opposite direction. They tip their caps in greeting and we nod in response. "We've heard that they are planning to use them to bomb Britain. They're faster and more maneuverable than zeppelins and much easier to navigate. Twenty of them dropping bombs on London at once would cause horrific damage."

The night I stood and watched the zeppelin raid over London, the streets were filled with people transfixed by the display. What would it be like if bombs were raining from the sky like hailstones?

"Is that possible?" I ask, horrified.

"Keep your voice down," Amelie warns. "Anything is possible. Certainly the Germans are building new airfields around Ghent and modifying old ones. At Gontrode, they're building new hangars that aren't large enough for zeppelins, so they must be for something else. What they are for is the secret we must discover."

"How can I help with that?"

We're almost at the hospital now, and Amelie slows down and pretends to be interested in some ducks swimming on the canal. "The work at Gontrode could be to prepare it as a base for Gotha raids on England. Our contact there—she works in the cafeteria and picks up a lot of gossip—has said that the Germans seem to be preparing for something to arrive. As soon as that happens, we will need someone to go down there and take a look, and maybe some photographs."

"Inside the airfield?" I ask nervously.

"No, just observing from outside to watch the new aircraft arrive."

"I'll do it," I say without hesitation. "But I don't have a camera."

Amelie reaches into the pannier on her bicycle, picks out a small package wrapped like a sandwich and hands it to me. "Pretend this is part of your lunch," she says as we enter the hospital grounds, "but don't open it until you get home. Practice with it and you will receive instructions about when to use it in a day or two."

I quickly stuff the package in my bag beside my real lunch as we park our bikes and go to our respective wards. The day drags by and I can't stop thinking about the camera. It's like carrying a bomb that might explode at any second.

As soon as I get home, I go to my room and carefully unwrap the package to reveal an aluminum camera only slightly larger than a pack of playing cards. The front pulls out and there's a small viewfinder to see what you're photographing. It's called a Vest Pocket Kodak, and it's loaded with film and comes with a slim instruction manual in English. I read the manual and practice with the camera without actually taking a picture. Then I hide it under the clothes in my dresser drawer and go to bed.

I lie awake wondering when I will receive my instructions—half of me hoping I won't have to wait long, the other half hoping I never hear anything more. For the first time, I feel like a real spy.

It's a scary feeling.

Chapter 7

Giants—April 7, 1917

I drag myself out of bed and haul on my clothes hours before dawn. I was so terrified I wouldn't wake up in time that I didn't sleep a wink. Yesterday, the scrap of paper with my instructions was tucked behind the cistern. It told me that the first Gotha bombers are to arrive at dawn this morning, and it's my job to photograph them. This means that I have to cycle to Gontrode, a journey of more than two hours in the dark.

Last evening, I told Mama that I had an early shift at the hospital so she wouldn't wonder where I was when she woke up. I'll be breaking curfew on a route that my permit doesn't allow, but if I'm stopped I'll say I'm just taking a pannier of vegetables to my old grandmother in Ghent and need to get back to the hospital in time to nurse the wounded German sailors there. That'll probably work —unless whoever stops me becomes suspicious and looks beneath the potatoes and onions, where the camera is hidden.

I slip downstairs as quietly as possible and open the front door. A huge full moon is hanging just above the western horizon, casting its eerie silver light over everything. I'm so entranced by it that I almost fall over Florien, who is smoking on the step. I had heard him stumble in late last night but had no idea he was up already.

"Where're you off to?" he asks, standing up. "Don't you know there's a curfew on?"

"I have an early shift at the hospital. A load of wounded came in yesterday. What are you doing up at this time?"

"Couldn't sleep," he says with a shrug. "I have to go to work soon too." His cigarette glows a deep red as he takes a long drag on it. He looks tired and sad. "Beautiful, isn't it?" he says, looking up at the moon. "Do you remember how Papa used to wrap us up in blankets and take us out at night to show us the stars—the Great Bear, Cassiopeia."

"I do." I'm torn between my need to get to Gontrode before dawn and a desire to stay and talk with Florien. "Orion, the Hunter, was my favourite. He never came up very high in the sky, as if he was hiding over the horizon, stalking his prey." I look at the sky, anxiously aware that I have to leave. "I have to hurry or I'll be late."

I move to step past Florien, but he puts a hand out and rests it on my shoulder. "Do you miss Papa?" he asks softly.

His gesture is gentle and his voice wistful. This is the first time he's spoken about Papa since I returned home, and the only glimpse he's given of the sensitive boy I knew before the war. Why must he start opening up when I have to go?

"Of course I miss Papa," I say, more abruptly than I intend. "And I will always hate the Germans for killing him."

I feel Florien's hand tense on my shoulder. "You blame everything on them," he says, the softness in his voice fading. "You haven't been here for two years. You ran away to live comfortably and safely. You don't understand the Germans. They're strong, and when they split this weak country into its two rightful parts, we will be strong as well. If the French and British would only recognize that they cannot win, then all the killing would stop."

"I'm sorry, Florien," I say. "I didn't mean to upset you."

My brother stares hard at me for a moment. He removes his hand, drops his cigarette and crushes it under his boot. As he turns away, he says under his breath, "In any case, it wasn't the Germans who killed Papa."

"What do you mean it wasn't the Germans?" I say. "They lined him up in the square with the others and shot him."

"Never mind," Florien snarls over his shoulder as he stomps off into the darkness. "You don't understand. You never will."

Totally confused by the encounter, I pull my bicycle out from beside the house and set off. I'm both upset by Florien and annoyed that I missed an opportunity to re-establish some kind of relationship with him. He's so touchy. Half the time he's my sensitive younger brother, and half the time he's an unpleasant devotee of all things German. I try to establish a connection with him, but I realize it is partly so that I can find out information about the U-boat docks, and that makes me feel guilty. I'm using my own brother. I want him to open up to me, but only so I can get information from him. And there's no way I can ever open up to him.

Feeling miserable, I head out onto the tree-lined country roads as the moon sets and the pre-dawn darkness thickens. It makes cycling difficult, but I'm glad that it will also make it harder for any German patrols to spot me. As it turns out, the roads I travel are completely deserted and I make good time.

As I cycle through the darkness, I find myself thinking of Alec. This must be a bit like his world in the tunnels below the war, except that I can breathe fresh air and feel the breeze on my face.

"I hope you're all right," I say softly, "although I don't know where you are or if you're even still alive." It feels oddly comforting to speak to him. "I'm a real spy now, furtively cycling through the dark with a hidden camera and a mission to photograph a secret plane. I wish you were here so I could tell you all about it—but that's not possible. You have your war and I have mine."

I have memorized a map that shows me the route around the edge of Ghent and down to Gontrode. The two-and-a-half-hour journey goes quickly and I soon find myself in the small wood from which I should be able to see the airfield and photograph the

Gothas when they come in to land. I hide my bicycle deep among the trees, retrieve my camera from the pannier and work my way forward just as the sky behind me turns red with the rising sun.

As the light grows, the airfield materializes out of the darkness. Beyond the trees, a swath of open ground stretches away to a high chain fence. At first, I can see nothing beyond the fence but a farmer's field, but then I notice that the grass is carefully groomed —it's a runway.

The only airfield I've ever seen is the one I took off from in December, and it was little more than a cow paddock with a row of tents and a couple of barn-like buildings where the planes were stored and repaired. Gontrode is very different. Over to my left, at least half a mile away, is the building where I assume the airfield workers and zeppelin crews live. It's a three-story brick structure as long as one side of the market square in Damme. There are lights in several of the windows.

Big as that building is, it's dwarfed by the two vast structures beside it. Even at this distance they are impressive. Each is too large to fit in the main square in Bruges and would tower over the surrounding buildings. Huge sliding doors cap the ends nearest to me. They must house the monstrous zeppelins that I saw over London. Once I can drag my eyes from them, I see that there are two smaller buildings farther away. I wonder if these are for the airplanes I'm here to photograph.

As I peer across the field in the brightening day, I notice tiny figures in front of the farthest of the small hangars. They're pushing open large doors on the end of the building, revealing the dark cavern within. I peer to try to make out what the figures are doing, wishing I had a pair of binoculars. Their activity seems random at first, but as I watch, several of them turn and look directly at me.

A lance of fear runs through me as I think I've been spotted, but the figures are pointing into the sky. Then I hear a deep rumble. It grows until it's coming from directly above me. It feels as if the sky is about to collapse on my head. I look up where the trees are thinnest.

The massive plane has two engines situated between the wings, one on each side of the square fuselage. It's so low in the sky that the wind from the propellers is waving the tops of the trees and I can see the evil-looking bombs slung underneath. I stare open-mouthed as the Gotha bomber drops onto the grass runway and bounces away toward the hangar, where the waiting men move forward to greet it. My mind whirls with images of what damage the bomb load of one of these monsters could do. And what destruction could ten, twenty, fifty of these horrors wreak on London in a single night? If the woman I saw on that London street called the zeppelin's baby killers, what would she call these?

As I hear the engines of the second bomber coming in over my head, I open my camera. When the plane fills the viewfinder, I click the shutter. I take more shots as the third and fourth bomber fly over me, drop onto the runway and move toward the hangar. But in my eagerness to get a good shot, I have stepped out of the trees. As I look up from the camera, I see activity as the planes arrive outside the hangar. I think I can make out a figure with binoculars. My heart starts racing—he is looking straight at me.

Other figures are beginning to move across the airfield in my direction. They're a long way off, but I must hurry if I'm to escape. Then I hear the noise of a fifth plane, deeper and louder than before. I look up and gasp as I'm engulfed in the shadow of something from a nightmare.

The plane thundering over my head is at least twice the size of the immense Gothas.

Chapter 8

Escape—April 7, 1917

I stare in awe as the monster drops down and lands. The tail alone is the size of an entire plane that flew me into Belgium. The vast wing and fuselage area is covered in a lozenge-shaped camouflage pattern painted with black German crosses. I can see five crewmen in open turrets, and there must be at least another two inside the enclosed cockpit. I snap picture after picture until the film won't wind anymore. Then I notice that the figures coming toward me are much closer—and they're running now.

Clutching my tiny camera, I plunge back into the trees as the first shot rings out and a bullet crashes through the branches above my head. I tear my way through the underbrush, praying that I can remember exactly where I left my bicycle. Fortunately, I almost fall over it. I stop for a moment to listen for the sounds of pursuit, but I'm not sure I could hear anything over my thumping heart and ragged breathing. I try to close my camera, but my hands are shaking so much that I keep dropping it. Eventually, I simply stuff in it my pannier under the vegetables. It makes little difference. If I'm found with a camera—open or closed—I'll be put against a wall and shot. Oddly, despite the thoughts whirling through my head, I don't feel scared. I'm in mortal danger, but my mind is working incredibly fast, weighing various choices and making decisions. There are not many options.

I push my bicycle out of the trees and pedal for all I'm worth. The road is frighteningly straight. If the Germans decide to come looking for me, I won't be hard to spot. And almost as soon as I think this, I hear the distant rumble of a truck. Without thinking, I swerve off the road onto the nearest farm track. My front wheel catches in a rut and I fly over the handlebars and land painfully in a ditch. My bicycle lands on top of me and I lie still, hoping I can't be seen from the road.

The rumble of the truck grows until it almost deafens me, and then it fades into the distance. I lie still until my breathing returns to something close to normal, and then I wonder what I'm going to do.

I'm lucky to have escaped this long. Obviously I have stumbled on something important and secret. Not even Amelie's contact at the airfield knew the giant plane was coming in this morning. And the Germans now know that someone has seen their new weapon. They may not know I've taken pictures of it, but they certainly know I ran away. They will be searching the roads all day for a lone girl on foot or on a bicycle—and when they find her, they will execute her.

I lie in the ditch for what seems an age, worrying. I've never been more frightened. At least that's what I think before I hear the clop of horse's hooves and the creak of wagon wheels coming down the farm track. I'll be in plain sight to anyone passing along the track, but I don't move. There's no point. I've nowhere to run to.

The cart stops beside me and deep voice says, "Bonjour, jeune femme."

I push the bicycle off me, sit up and say, "Good morning." The speaker is a bewhiskered old man in a peasant shirt and cloth cap. He's sitting on the seat of a rough two-wheeled cart, holding the reins of an equally aged draft horse. Both the man and the horse are looking at me curiously. "I fell off my bicycle," I add.

The old man nods as if what I have said is explanation enough for finding a strange girl and her bicycle in his ditch. I haul myself painfully to my feet.

"You are injured?" the man asks.

"Just bruised from my fall," I say.

"Perhaps, then, I may offer you a ride somewhere in my cart. It's not very fancy and Monsieur Éclair is by no means as quick as the noisy trucks that the Boches rush around in, but it may get you where you need to go. My name is Étienne Dumont."

"Thank you," I say. "You're very kind. My name is Manon Wouters, but I'm going quite far, to Damme."

With surprising agility, Étienne climbs down from the cart. "I think I may be able to go that way," he says, grabbing my bicycle.

"A moment, please," I say. There's no point in trying to hide anything from this man. I take my camera out of the pannier and close it.

Étienne stares. I'm about to stuff the camera in my pocket when he says, "Better give it to me."

I hesitate for a moment, but I have to trust this man. I give him the camera. Étienne wedges it under Monsieur Éclair's broad harness. There's a flap of leather there, like a small pocket. I have no time to ask what he normally hides there before he heaves my bicycle into the back of the cart, pulls hay and sacks of turnips and potatoes around it to make it look as if it has been there for some time, and helps me up onto the seat beside him. With a bit of encouragement, Monsieur Éclair hauls us off the track and onto the road.

We haven't gone far when we come upon the Germans. A gray truck is blocking the road, and three soldiers hold their rifles at the ready and watch us approach.

"Let me talk," Étienne murmurs out of the corner of his mouth as the soldiers raise their rifles and order us to halt. "*Guten Morgen*," he says cheerfully as Monsieur Éclair draws to a halt.

The corporal, a boy barely older than Florien, steps forward. "Down," he orders.

Étienne and I climb down and stand beside the cart. I'm shaking with fear, but Étienne is a picture of calm.

"How can we help you?" he asks in flawless German.

"Where are you going?" the corporal asks.

"I'm taking my produce to the market in Bruges."

"It's a long way. Ghent is closer," the corporal points out.

"Indeed it is," Étienne agrees with a smile. "But your naval colleagues at the dockyards are better paid than you, so prices are higher. Besides, I am taking my niece home." He waves a hand at me. "She has been staying on the farm for the past week and her mother is missing her."

"Let me see your papers," the corporal orders.

Étienne and I hand over our identity papers and the corporal examines them closely. While he's doing this, the other two soldiers poke their way through the produce in the cart. I keep my eyes fixed firmly on the ground at my feet, scared that my expression will give me away if I look at the corporal.

The two soldiers jump down from the cart. "Nothing there," one of them says.

"We must search you," the corporal says.

"Of course. You must do your job thoroughly," Étienne says amiably.

The two soldiers pat us down and go through the pockets of our clothes. I try not to think about what would have happened if the camera had been there.

Eventually, the search is done, but the corporal seems in no hurry to let us proceed. He strolls over to Monsieur Éclair and strokes his flank. "A good animal," he says appreciatively. "I grew up on a farm in Württemberg. We had draft horses like this one."

"Monsieur Éclair is a Percheron," Étienne explains proudly. "He is descended from the horses ridden by the Roman legions, and his ancestors carried knights into battle five hundred years ago."

The corporal seems interested, but his hand is stroking Monsieur Éclair's neck mere inches from where my camera is hidden. I want to break away and run for the nearby trees, but Étienne has more nerve than me.

"I'm sure you and your men could use some fresh vegetables," he says, lifting a sack out of the cart and holding it out to the corporal. "And I think you may find a couple of bottles of good Belgian beer to wash them down with."

The corporal hesitates for a moment, then steps toward us and accepts the sack. "Thank you," he says. He gives Monsieur Éclair a final appreciative pat on the rump. "On your way, then."

We climb up onto the cart. And I struggle to force myself to look as relaxed and casual as Étienne. We wave at the soldiers who wave back, and Monsieur Éclair resumes his plodding pace.

"That was close," I say when we're a safe distance away.

Étienne shrugs as if it's no big deal. "You were taking pictures of the big plane that came over this morning?" he asks.

"How did you know?"

He laughs. "Handsome though he is, I didn't think you were here to photograph Monsieur Éclair, especially with such a small camera. Besides, I saw the plane fly over a short while before I found you in my ditch."

"You're taking a big risk in helping me," I point out.

Again Étienne shrugs. "The Boches like a bottle of good beer now and then. We're lucky that our country is famous for brewing. And I'm lucky that I have had a good winter crop this year. The Boches took almost all my harvest last year. Besides, my son is fighting them in the tiny corner of our country that is still free. I don't like to think of monsters like that plane dropping bombs on him."

We come upon no more roadblocks and the journey north mostly unfolds in companionable silence, lulled by Monsieur Éclair's steady clopping. It's late afternoon when Étienne drops me where the road turns off for Damme, and I've completely missed my shift at the hospital.

"Will you be able to cycle?" Étienne asks as he retrieves my camera and hands it to me.

"If I take it easy," I reply, sliding the camera into my pocket. "I can't thank you enough. You saved my life." I lean over and kiss him on the cheek.

He simply smiles, wishes me luck, climbs back on his cart and encourages Monsieur Éclair on their way to Bruges. Gingerly, I mount my bicycle and slowly head home.

Chapter 9

Final Break—April 7, 1917

I tell Mama that my bruises are from a fall at the hospital and she fusses over me and orders me to go and lie down. I do as I'm told because I need to rest and I need to think.

I am incredibly lucky. Without Étienne, I would be undergoing interrogation in prison now—or worse. What I'm doing now is more than the dangerous game Major Macleod warned me about— it's a matter of life and death. I think over the mistakes I made today. It was being awestruck by the size of the planes that made me step out of the shelter of the trees and allowed the soldier with the binoculars to see me. I must not let my emotions get the better of me. I think about how scared I was at the roadblock and how calm Étienne was. At all times, I must have a convincing story ready to explain where I am, where I've been and where I'm going. And I must find a better hiding place for my camera. Perhaps I could put a false bottom in my pannier.

None of this will guarantee my safety, but it will increase my chances of surviving to get the information I discover to where it will do the most good.

This last thought reminds me of the photographs I have taken. I was supposed to give the film to Amelie at the hospital, but I was so late back that I missed her. I take the camera out of my pocket, rewind the film and remove it according to the instructions. It's a small canister—much easier to hide than the entire camera. I will take it in and give it to Amelie tomorrow. I hide the camera and the roll of film at the bottom of my clothes drawer, lie back down on the bed and, for the hundredth time, think back over my first real experience of spying.

I must have dozed off, because I'm jerked awake by the sound of Florien's voice in the kitchen. I rub my eyes. It's still light outside, so Florien is home unusually early. I think back to our conversation this morning on the step. Perhaps I can recapture the connection we had then. I smooth my clothes and head through to the kitchen.

Mama is standing by the stove, looking worried and wiping her hands on her apron. Florien is leaning on the table, his brow furrowed in anger.

"It's a disgrace," he says as I enter the room.

"What's a disgrace?" I ask as cheerfully as I can manage.

Florien looks up. "It'll probably make you happy," he sneers. "The Americans have declared war on Germany."

I'm speechless. I want to shout for joy. This means the end of the war! Germany cannot possibly win against Britain, France, Russia and the industrial might of America. Belgium will be free again!

I'm struggling to think of something to say that won't offend Florien when he speaks again. "It's none of their business. They should stay at home and not interfere in things that don't concern them and they don't understand."

I can't stop myself from asking, "Didn't the Germans make it their concern when the U-boats began sinking American ships?"

I expect Florien to explode, but he speaks calmly. "Is it fair that American businesses can make a fortune loading their ships with goods that they can sell freely to Britain and France, while Germany is prevented from buying anything because of the British naval blockade—a blockade that is in violation of international law? Why do you think we're starving in Belgium?"

"We Belgians are starving," I reply, keeping my voice low and even, "because the Germans take everything for themselves. They took most of the harvest last fall."

"Hard decisions must be made in war," Florien says with a shrug. It's frightening how calmly he is speaking. It's as if stealing food from an entire country—and all the suffering that causes—is of no concern to him. "More U-boats are putting to sea every day. Britain will feel what it's like to starve before the summer is over. And even if Britain and France keep fighting, America cannot be ready for war for at least a year. Russia is close to collapse; the Czar abdicated last month and there is revolution on the streets. Once Russia is defeated, the entire might of the German army will fall on the French and the British. The war will be over before the first American soldier steps off a ship in Europe."

There's a smile on his lips and a fanatical glint in his eyes. I half expect him to snap to attention and salute. His pompous certainty is infuriating.

"How can you believe that?" I ask, struggling to keep my voice even. I risked my life today, and the fear I felt at seeing that giant bomber and surviving the German roadblock is bubbling beneath the surface, building a pressure that must be released. "It's madness to trust the Germans! They invaded us even though they had signed a treaty declaring that we were a neutral country." As I think of what the Germans have done, my anger swells and my voice rises. "They have destroyed our country to feed their war machine. They deliberately burned the library at Leuven; they killed hundreds of women and children in Dinant."

As I talk, the rage within me grows. I have been hiding my hatred too long. Now I can't keep it bottled up anymore, so I lash out at the only target available. "You think the Germans are honourable people, forced into doing bad things by the war. You couldn't be more wrong. They don't care for anyone but themselves, and they will do whatever they can to achieve their own ends. You and your drinking friends foolishly believe that the Germans, who have committed unspeakable atrocities in our country, will somehow create a free Flemish state. It's a fantasy—a dangerous fantasy that will never be reality."

I know I should stop before I say something that will create an unbridgeable gulf between us, but I can't. My hatred—the hatred I promised Major Macleod I could keep under control—has got hold of me and tears of frustration, rage and fear are streaming down my cheeks.

"You admire German power, but it's destructive power. It has destroyed our country and taken thousands of our people. German power killed our father. I will never forgive them for that. How can you?"

I stand across the kitchen table from Florien, my arms hanging limply by my sides, tears dripping onto the kitchen floor. I am emotionally drained. I expect to be assaulted by Florien's angry words as he attempts to defend himself. Instead, I am met by silence. My brother is staring down at the table, his face an image of sadness. He blinks back his own tears and swallows heavily. I see the little boy I comforted when his favourite toy broke or when he woke up in the night after a bad dream.

"Florien, I'm sorry," I say as I step around the table. I want nothing more than to give him a hug and recapture the relationship we had before this war damaged us, but as I approach, his body tenses and his fists clench. When he looks up, he's so full of anger that I stop mid-step.

For an age we stand and stare at each other. I realize that the person opposite me is not my brother but a fanatical stranger I don't know. I'm struggling to think of something to say when Florien turns on his heel, strides across the floor and throws open the front door.

"Florien!" I call after him, but he's gone.

I look over at Mama, who hasn't moved from the stove and is staring at the empty doorway, still obsessively wiping her hands on her apron.

"I'm sorry, Mama," I say.

She looks over at me as if noticing me for the first time. "Don't be sorry, Manon," she says gently. "None of this is your fault. Florien has chosen his path. It's a path that's distorted by your father's death and this damnable war, but there is nothing we can do to change that."

I go over to Mama and we hug each other. We are still standing like that when I hear a tentative knock on the door and a familiar voice asking, "Is everything all right?"

I look up to see Amelie framed in the doorway.

"Family argument," I say as casually as I can. "My brother, Florien, and I disagree about a number of things."

"Was that Florien who almost knocked me over in the street a moment ago?" she asks. "He seems angry."

I nod in response to both Amelie's question and her statement. "Come in. Mama, this is Amelie, my friend from the hospital."

"Pleased to meet you," Mama says, stepping forward and offering a spotlessly clean hand in greeting. "Manon has told me such a lot about you. Let me put the kettle on."

"Thank you," Amelie says, "but I can't stay. I was just passing by and saw the door open, so I looked in to see if everything was okay." She stares at me intently and tilts her head to suggest that I join her outside.

"I'll walk you to the corner," I say, picking up on the hint. "I won't be long, Mama."

As soon as we're outside, Amelie asks, "You never came to the hospital. What went wrong?"

I tell her about my day as we walk to the end of the street.

"You were lucky the old farmer found you," she says. "It's comforting to know that there are still good, brave people around. Do you have the film you took?"

"It's hidden in my room."

"Good. Bring it to the hospital tomorrow. But leave the camera at home. It'll be safer there, and we may need it again." She stops and turns to face me. "You did well, Manon."

"Thank you. I was really scared when the Germans stopped us on the road."

"I'm not surprised. But that's what makes us brave—being scared and overcoming the fear. I'll see you tomorrow. Get a good rest. You've earned it."

Amelie turns and sets off toward the market square. I walk slowly back home, my mind filled with emotions. I hope I can get a good rest. I certainly need it after the turmoil of the day.

Chapter 10

An Unpleasant Surprise—April 8, 1917

I sleep well, but memories of the previous day overwhelm me the moment I open my eyes, hauling me back down into worry and despair. I try to appear cheerful with Mama over my breakfast slice of bread, but I can see she hasn't slept much. Florien didn't return home last night, and Mama is clearly fretting about where he's been.

I collect the film canister and wait for Amelie at our usual spot in the market square. When she doesn't show up, I'm not worried— she sometimes goes to the hospital early—and I set off along the canal into Bruges.

The morning is crisp and clear, and the birds are busy calling to one another and building nests in the trees along the canal towpath. The fresh air blows away some of the misery in my mind, and an image of Alec pops unbidden into my head. "You'd be proud of me," I say under my breath. "I overcame my fear and achieved something important yesterday. That's what I came here to do."

It's stupid talking to this boy I barely knew, but it makes me strangely happy as I cycle up to the hospital and park my bicycle. Then I see Amelie standing by the steps.

"What happened?" I ask, horrified at how she looks.

She's limping as she steps forward to greet me. Her left arm is in a sling, and there's a large, livid purple bruise on her cheek. Amelie attempts a reassuring smile, but it obviously hurts.

"I was beaten up after I left you last night," she explains.

"How are you?" I ask scanning her injuries.

"I ache a bit, but it's mostly just bruising—except for this." She pats her sling with her healthy hand. "Seems I landed on my wrist awkwardly. It's a bad sprain or a minor fracture. Either way, I won't be cycling too far for a while."

"Who did this?"

"A bunch of thugs—kids, mostly. It was my own stupidity. I saw them lounging at a street corner. I should have turned and gone home another way, but you'd been so brave that day, I thought I should be as well. At first it was just a few shouted comments, but then one boy said I was a spy."

"How did he know?" I ask, horrified.

Amelie shrugs and grimaces in pain. "I don't think he did, but we live in a small town, Manon. We can keep secrets from the Germans, but it's hard to keep secrets from family and neighbours. The boy lives on my street, so he knows how I feel about the Germans, and he's seen me come and go at odd hours. He may suspect something, but I think he was just trying to show off in front of his friends. Anyway, things escalated from there and here I am."

"I should have walked with you all the way home."

"Then we'd both have been beaten up. I'll recover soon enough." She moves closer to me and lowers her voice. "The problem is, I'm supposed to deliver the film to Pieter in Maldegem this evening, but since I can't cycle, I have no way of getting there."

"I'll go," I say immediately.

"I was hoping you'd say that." She looks relieved. "Are you certain you're up to it after yesterday?"

"I'm fine. A few sore muscles, that's all. I'll go straight after my shift this afternoon. What's Pieter's address?"

Amelie produces a scrap of paper from her sling and I stuff it in my pocket.

"Pieter has connections with people who can smuggle things over the border into Holland," she explains, "and from there onto an English fishing boat."

"Pieter's a smuggler?"

Amelie attempts another smile. "I know—a policeman who smuggles. These are strange times indeed! Thank you for doing this. I've just been to see Matron and she told me to take a few days off work, so I should be getting home."

"How will you get back?"

"A farmer bringing in an order of vegetables gave me a lift this morning. He's going back soon, so I must go and find him."

We've finished talking, but Amelie makes no move to go.

"Is there anything else?" I ask.

My friend nods. "I've thought a lot about whether I should tell you this, but I think you have to know."

"What?"

"Your brother was one of my attackers. He didn't join in—just stood back and watched—but he didn't try to stop the others. I'm sorry."

Amelie limps away and leaves me standing on the hospital steps. I'm stunned. How can this be? I know I raged at Florien's stupid ideas yesterday. I know he's angry and horribly misguided. But being part of a gang that beats up a woman on the street! What has happened to the little brother I once knew?

~~~~~

I struggle through the day as best I can, trying not to let my fury at Florien burst out. The German soldiers I talk to are the enemy, but they're also helpless. They signed up or were drafted to fight for their country, and now they're caught up in the same madness as soldiers from any other nation. But Florien's not helpless. He's making choices about what side he's on, and it's the side that beat up my friend.

At the end of my shift, I cycle down to Maldegem to deliver the film to Pieter. I often work longer than my regular shift, so I know Mama won't worry if I'm not home on time. And I should be back well before dark.

Pieter meets me at his door. He's surprised to see me, but I explain what happened to Amelie, without mentioning Florien's involvement. He leads me into his kitchen, where we sit while I tell him of my adventures at Gontrode and pass him the film canister.

"This old farmer, Étienne Dumont, was very helpful," Pieter says when I have finished.

"He saved my life."

Pieter scratches his chin thoughtfully. "Do you think he would help us? It might be useful to have another contact, or as you discovered, a refuge near the airfield."

"I'm sure he would help," I say.

"Perhaps another bicycle trip down to Gontrode is in order," Pieter suggests. "You've done very well, Manon."

"Thank you," I say, feeling a surge of pride.

"There may be more work to do around this giant new airplane, but first I must get this film and your report safely out of the country. I'll be in contact when I hear back, probably in a day or two."

I nod agreement, although the thought of going back to Gontrode doesn't thrill me. Then something Pieter said hits me.

"A day or two? How can you possibly get my film and report to Britain and receive a response that soon? Amelie said the film must be smuggled across the border and then put on a fishing boat to England. That must take days."

"It does," Pieter says with a grin, "but only the film has to go that way. We have a much faster way to send messages. Let me show you."

Intrigued, I follow him out his back door and past his vegetable plots. He lives on the edge of town, and the back of his property is heavily wooded. I see that we are headed for a wooden shed among the trees.

Pieter opens the door and ushers me in. I'm met by a strong, acrid smell and the sound of nervous fluttering. As my eyes adjust to the dark, I begin to make out a row of wire cages with tiny, beady eyes glinting out of them.

"Homing pigeons," Pieter says proudly. "I have only a few and I have to keep them secret. But I can put short coded messages in canisters attached to their legs and they will deliver them to the British."

"But surely they can't fly all the way to England and back?"

"They could, but they don't have to. We have a wireless transmitter just across the border in Holland. The pigeons fly there and the message is sent on."

"Wouldn't it be simpler to have the wireless transmitter here?" I ask.

"Simpler, yes, but much less secure. The Germans put a lot of effort into listening to radio messages. Mostly, they are trying to work out what the British navy and army are doing, but they would soon pick up my signals and that would be the end. Holland is neutral, so the Germans can't do anything about transmitters there."

"Clever," I say admiringly. "So my report will go out tonight?"

"As soon as I get it coded. They'll have it in London by midnight. I suspect they'll quickly make a decision on what to do next."

I imagine Major Macleod sitting at his desk with Pieter's decoded message. I wonder if he'll know the information's from me.

"Will they want me to go back to Gontrode?" I ask.

"Quite possibly, so be ready."

We leave the pigeons in peace and return to the house.

"Do you live here alone?" I ask.

"I do," Pieter says. "This is my parents' house, but they fled to Holland when the Germans invaded. They're living with my wife's family there. The pigeons were my father's hobby, so it was easy to set up that link in the communications network."

"Your wife went to Holland as well?" I ask.

Pieter's face clouds with sadness. "My wife's dead," he says. "She was killed when the war was only a few weeks old. She was in the town square when a shell exploded nearby."

"I'm sorry," I say. "The Germans killed my father as well."

"It wasn't a German shell. It was French."

I'm dumbfounded. I know what it's like to have someone you love killed by the enemy. How much worse must it be to have that someone killed by friends?

"These things happen in war. Once a shell is fired, only God can decide where it falls," Pieter says with a shrug. "Anyway, you should probably be heading back." He's making an obvious effort to sound brighter. "Don't forget to pass on my best wishes to Amelie. I hope she recovers soon."

"I'll do that."

At the front door, Pieter asks, "Have you heard the good news?"

"About America joining the war? Yes, it's wonderful."

"It is," Pieter agrees, "but it won't change things in the short term. In fact, it might make things worse. The Germans must know that they cannot win once the Americans are here, so they will redouble their efforts to finish the war before that can happen. I suspect it will be a very hard year or two for everyone, and that will make our work here that much more important."

"I'll do whatever is necessary," I say.

Pieter smiles. "I have no doubts on that score, Manon. Again, well done. I'll be in touch."

We shake hands. Pieter closes his door, and I mount my bicycle and begin the journey home.

For the first part of the ride back to Damme, I feel happier than I have in days. I'm proud of what I have done and glad that Pieter is happy with my work. I have successfully undertaken my first assignment, braved danger and survived. "Well, Alec," I murmur, "now I'm making an important contribution."

As I approach home, however, gloomy thoughts of Florien begin to intrude into my mind. Who has my brother become? I can forgive him many things—I can explain away his admiration for the Germans as the effects of this dreadful war on an impressionable, sensitive boy, and I can hope that he will once more see sense when it's all over. But I cannot forgive him for last night. Even if he took no active part in what happened to Amelie, how could he stand by and watch while she was beaten? I'm almost glad that Papa is not around to see what Florien has become.

Chapter 11

Back to Gontrode—April 29, 1917

A pril is cold and unusually snowy, which means there are few bombing raids. I struggle to keep warm as I cycle to work and spend much of my spare time collecting firewood from the nearby woods. I continue to gather what information I can from wounded soldiers and sailors and pass it on.

Amelie returns to work a couple of days after my journey to see Pieter. Physically, she has recovered quickly, and her wrist is only sprained. Emotionally, the beating has left deeper scars, and she often seems distant and preoccupied. My dangerous game. is becoming more dangerous every day—and there is no end in sight.

I avoid Florien as much as possible and respond to him only when absolutely necessary. Mama begs me to talk more to him, to try to engage with him and draw him back into the family that he seems to be slipping away from, but I cannot. It takes all my energy not to berate him violently for allowing Amelie to be beaten.

I bury myself in work at the hospital, volunteering for extra shifts and staying a way from home as much as possible. A few days ago, a young German naval officer was admitted. He was wounded in an air raid on the Bruges dockyards and the doctors have spent hours removing dozens of pieces of shrapnel from the right side of his body, but his worst wound is where a flying piece of bomb hit him in the head.

At first, the officer sleeps most of the time, tossing and turning and crying out as if he's reliving the horror he has been through. When he's awake, he lies staring at the ceiling. I mop his fevered brow when he's in one of his deliriums, and feed and bathe him when he's awake. He responds to commands and eats when I spoon-feed him.

Nursing the German officer only increases my confusion. His name is Manfred, and he's young and polite and grateful for any help I give him. His head is bandaged, but I can see fair hair sticking out from under his dressing. His eyes are a startling blue and light up whenever he smiles. He seems vaguely familiar, but I have no idea where I might have seen him before.

I cannot see him as an enemy. He's just a young man damaged by this dreadful war. The other nurses tell me that he screamed most of the previous night, but when I arrive to change the dressings on his wound, he's much better and is sitting up in bed.

"You're very kind," he says as I work.

"It's my job," I reply.

"But you have gentle hands and you genuinely care for your patients, even though we are your enemy."

"Bombs and shells don't distinguish between friends and enemies," I point out. "Armies are simply made up of boys who thought they were doing the right thing. I wish you Germans would go home, but I'm certain that you are not personally responsible for invading my country."

"I too wish I could go home," Manfred confides. "I come from a military family. I'm the product of a line of men who fought for Frederick the Great and with Field Marshal Blücher at Waterloo, so there was never the slightest doubt where I would end up. My older brother joined the army, so to be different, I went into the navy. I thought this war would be my chance to be a hero. I imagined my brother marching triumphantly through the streets of Paris while I swept the arrogant British fleet from the high seas.

Instead, my brother was blown to pieces by a British shell at the Somme, and I have lost every friend I joined up with."

"How did you get wounded?" I ask.

Manfred is silent so long that I think he's refusing to answer. I've finished changing his dressing when at last he begins to speak softly.

"A year ago, I was first officer on the light cruiser Arachne when we hit a mine off the coast of Denmark. The Arachne sank in minutes. I survived with only minor injuries, but I spent what seemed like hours in the sea, listening to my shipmates scream as the ship rolled over and trapped them in air pockets that slowly filled with water. When they pulled me to safety, those screams came with me and haunted my dreams.

"I spent several months in a hospital with the best of care. I improved but was judged unfit for command, so I was sent to Bruges to oversee construction in the docks. It was seen as a safe posting that would allow my nerves to recover." The young officer laughs bitterly. "Nothing is safe in this war. But I should count myself lucky—the man standing beside me when the bomb fell was never found."

Manfred stares out the window as if what he's describing is happening there. Tears are streaming down his cheeks and collecting in the stubble of his beard. He seems to have run out of energy.

"I'm sorry," he says.

"It's all right." I take his limp, pale hand and squeeze it. I get no response, so I collect the old dressings and leave. I feel sorry for Manfred and what he has gone through, but only one thing he said sticks in my mind, and it makes me wonder if I am losing my humanity. He said he was in charge of construction at the Bruges docks, and I can't help thinking how useful he could be.

I'm so deep in my thoughts that I don't notice Amelie approach until I feel her hurriedly stuff a piece of paper into the pocket of my uniform. "Tomorrow," she whispers as she passes me.

~~~~~

My instructions are straightforward: Étienne, the old farmer, has agreed to help us and I am to cycle down to his farm. At least this time my journey will be in daylight and I will be carrying nothing but a pannier of innocuous vegetables.

The danger will come that night.

I am to wait at Étienne's until dark, when he will give me two flares that Pieter has passed to him, one red and one green, and instructions on how to find a hole in the airfield fence. Our contact at Gontrode says that the giant plane is in one of the newly built, smaller hangars beside the Zeppelin sheds, and it is my job to mark that hangar. British bombers are planning to attack the airfield at ten thirty. I must be in position by then. When I hear the engines of the bombers, I will fire the red flare to guide them to the airfield. When they're overhead, I'll set off the green flare outside the hangar to mark where the giant bomber is. Then I'll escape in the confusion.

Sunset is at nine, so it won't be completely dark until after nine thirty, which doesn't give me much time to get into the airfield, cross it and prepare my flares. There's a waning half-moon tomorrow night, but it doesn't rise until well after midnight, so the darkness will cover me.

My journey down to Gontrode is uneventful and I spend much of the time talking to Alec inside my head, telling him of my adventures. I pray that one day I will be able to tell him my stories for real.

Étienne welcomes me with open arms. "I told Monsieur Éclair we would meet again," he says as he leads me into his kitchen, where a woman is taking a golden pie out of the oven. "This is my wife, Adelle. Can we offer you some pie?"

"It's kind of you," I say, smiling at Adelle, "but I don't think I could eat anything right now. My stomach is full of butterflies."

"It's very brave of you to come back here," Étienne says.

"It's very good of you to help," I reply.

He nods. "I am an old farmer—too old to fight. I must do what I can. Monsieur Éclair and I are at your service. But for now, we must wait. As soon as the sun goes down, I will lead you to the hole in the fence."

Étienne is as good as his word, and as twilight fades, we are standing in the trees close to where I took the photographs.

"That bush hides a hole in the wire," Étienne tells me, pointing out slightly darker patch by the fence. "Pull the loose wire to the side and you can slip through. The Germans don't patrol the perimeter very much and you'll be far enough away from the buildings that you will not be seen from there. Follow the fence around until you're behind the hangars. Then you simply wait until you hear the bombers."

Étienne digs in his pack and produces what looks like a small, squat pistol.

"This is your first flare," he explains. "Point it up in the air, flip the small switch at the back with your thumb and pull the trigger. The red flare will rise several hundred feet in the air to signal the airfield's location to the approaching bombers. This"—he pulls out a long stick with a pointed end—"is the green flare. Jam the pointed end in the ground and pull the flap at the top. Make sure you place it as close as possible to the hangar. It will burn very brightly once it starts, so make sure you get as far away as you can before anyone sees you."

"Thank you," I say. "I'll do the best I can."

"You'll do well. But don't linger. As soon as the bombing starts, it will be dangerous around the hangars, so hurry back to the fence. I'll be waiting for you. This may help."

Étienne hands me a short metal tube with a glass end.

"It's a flashlight." He turns away from the airfield and moves a tiny switch. A pale, narrow beam shines into the trees. "Don't use it unless you have to."

"Thank you," I say as I tuck the pistol and the flare into the belt of my skirt and slip the flashlight into my pocket.

"And now, I think it's dark enough to begin," Étienne says. "Good luck."

Chapter 12

Bombed—April 29, 1917

Even in the moonless dark, I feel like I'm trying to hide in broad daylight. As soon as I leave the shelter of the trees, I'm certain that anyone looking up from the hangars on the other side of the airfield will spot me immediately.

Crouching low and tripping over tree roots, I work my way to the fence, pull the gap in the wire open, squeeze through and feel my way around the edge of the airfield. I had assumed there would be little going on at night, but it seems I was wrong—lights flicker in the living quarters, and I begin to see figures moving in and out of the cones of light in front of the hangars.

I move as fast as I can until I am behind the hangars. Most of the work is going on at the front, so it's dark on my side. A worrying thought suddenly strikes me: What if the Germans are preparing the giant for a night flight? It might not even be here when the British bombers arrive, and everything will have been in vain.

There are four hangars, spaced widely apart—two towering zeppelin sheds and two smaller structures. I assume the smaller buildings house the Gothas and the giant bomber, but which is which? Pale rectangles of light shine through grubby windows at the back of each one. I take a deep breath and, in a crouching run, head across the open ground to the hangar at the near end of the row. I throw myself down beneath one of the windows and listen for the warning shouts and running boots I am certain will come.

But the only sounds are the officers barking orders, the clang of metal tools and my own heavy breathing. Carefully, I rise to my feet and peer through the bottom corner of the window.

The inside of the hangar is well lit with powerful lights on tall metal tripods, and despite the grime on the windowpane, I can clearly see the four Gotha bombers that must be the ones I watched land three weeks ago. They are parked, two on each side of the hangar. It's obvious that these planes won't be going anywhere tonight. Mechanics in greasy overalls are swarming over the machines closest to the hangar doors, and the engine of one is stripped and mostly in pieces on a sheet of canvas on the ground.

I hunch back down into the shadows, slide along the back wall, dart across the open space to the next hangar and squint through a corner of the window. There's only one plane in this hangar, but it takes up almost as much space as the four Gothas. It's parked side on to me, and although I'm standing on my tiptoes to peer in the window, I'm still looking at the underside of the lower wing. That wing is supported by a wooden tripods, and a stepladder leads up to a vast engine suspended between the two wings. There are propellers at both the front and the back of the engine, and a mechanic stands in a small cockpit between them and makes adjustments to a network of hoses running above his head.

I was awestruck by the size of the giant when it flew over me, but its size is mind-numbing this close up. I could stand on the lower wing, stretch my arms above my head and still not touch the upper wing. It's horrifying to think of the number of bombs this beast could carry to drop over innocent people's homes in London. It must be destroyed.

I'm about to move away when I see a German officer walk underneath the nose of the plane. He says something to the mechanic working on the engine and heads in my direction. I duck down before he can see me, but then I notice the door in the hangar wall. If the officer comes through that door, he will see me.

I run along the hangar wall and throw myself around the corner just as the light floods out the doorway. Keeping to the deepest shadows, I work my way forward, praying that this isn't the way the officer is planning on coming. In the last patch of shadow, I turn and peer back, but I can see very little in the darkness. There's no sign of the officer.

Looking the other way, I see a well-lighted scene of great activity. To my relief, most of the work is concentrated around the zeppelin shed, which towers above me like a dark mountain. The massive doors at the front are open and a zeppelin is sliding out into the light, dragged by a crowd of soldiers hauling on ropes. Men are shouting instructions all around, but the zeppelin moves in silence, giving the whole scene the eerie feel of a ghost story. I watch, transfixed, as the monster is drawn out into the open.

The first indication I have of the arrival of the British bombers is the sight of several men looking up and scanning the dark sky to the west. Then I hear the deep, distant rumble of the approaching planes. Others hear them as well, and groups of soldiers rush to drag wheeled carts with heavy machine guns mounted on top. At the far end of the runway, the harsh beam of a searchlight begins to sweep the sky.

There seems no point in firing the red flare—the searchlight is doing a better job of marking the airfield than I ever could—but I have to ignite the green flare to mark the position of the bomber. I try to haul the flare out of my waistband, but it's caught on something. I tug and the flare comes loose, but the flare gun also flies out and lands on the ground at my feet. It doesn't matter. I don't need the red flare. I jam the sharp end of the green flare in the ground and fumble for the tag I have to pull.

"*Was machen Sie?*"

A shudder of horror runs through me as I look up to see the silhouette of a figure coming toward me. Behind him the sausage-shaped zeppelin is almost out of the hangar. The sound of the approaching bombers is loud now. Soldiers are running about everywhere and the first of the machine guns opens up with a loud, staccato rattle.

"What are you doing?" the approaching man demands. "Who are you?" He's reaching for something in his belt. I have to stop him. Even if I manage to set off the green flare, he will be able to put it out. I fumble on the ground for the flare gun. The man is close now, and he's pulling a pistol out of a leather holster at his waist. I flip the switch on the flare gun as Étienne showed me, wave it at the man and pull the trigger.

There's a loud bang and something hisses within inches of the man's head. He stumbles back in surprise and turns. We both watch as the wavering red line ricochets off the wall of the hangar, traces a large, graceful arc and lands on top of the zeppelin. For a moment nothing happens, and then, with fascinating slowness, the red glow of the flare expands. It forms a widening circle of fire that eats hungrily down into the body of the airship.

People are beginning to point and look up. It's hard to believe how fast the flames are spreading, bursting out through the fabric walls and eating deep in the doomed vessel's heart. Above the growing roar of the inferno, the machine guns continue their rattling fire and the first bombs explode nearby. But the death of the zeppelin has everyone's attention now. The heat is becoming intense, hurting my cheeks, and people are beginning to run from the falling colossus. Even the man who discovered me is moving away from the heat.

The entire back end of the zeppelin is engulfed in flames and sagging to the ground in a mass of twisting metal. Sheets of burning fabric fly into the air like doomed birds as the fire races forward. The gondolas beneath the airship are crashing to the ground, and the terrified crewmen are scrambling away before the blazing giant falls on them.

I rip the top off the green flare, although I doubt it will do any good now, and run into the dark. When I reach the fence, I stop and look back. The skeleton of the zeppelin is largely hidden behind the massive shed, but flames from the wreck are still shooting high into the air. Half a dozen F.E.2bs are weaving around the airfield like moths round a candle flame. I can still hear the occasional bomb bursting and the German anti-aircraft guns. If I squint hard, I can just make out a green glow where I was huddled, but I have no idea whether the bombers have noticed it and I can see no obvious damage to the hangar housing the monstrous plane.

As I begin to follow the fence back to the gap, I notice that one of the F.E.2bs has peeled away and is flying to the north. I hold my breath as it wobbles toward the trees where Étienne is waiting for me, but at the last minute, the pilot manages to pull his machine up and it clears the trees and disappears from view.

By the time I reach the gap in the fence, the bombing raid is over and the flames from the zeppelin are dying down. There is a lot of activity around the hangars and the solitary searchlight is continuing its mournful sweeps of the empty sky. Was my mission a success? One of the dreaded zeppelins has been destroyed, but I don't know if any of the bombs hit either of the smaller hangars. The mission didn't turn out the way I thought it would, but I'm quickly learning that events in war rarely unfold as planned.

I begin to shiver violently, even though I'm wearing warm clothes and it's not a cold night. It must be the release of tension. Oddly, when I was in most danger, I was calmest. I thought rationally and rapidly about what I had to do and then did it. I didn't even hesitate to try to kill the man who interrupted me.

I begin laughing at the thought, quietly at first but soon uncontrollably. Tears run down my cheeks. I tried to kill a man. I probably did kill some people in the zeppelin. Me—a nurse who has dedicated her life to saving people, even enemy soldiers.

Eventually the hysterics pass and I regain control of my emotions. I wipe my face on my sleeve, slip through the fence and move into the trees.

"Étienne," I whisper. I'm back in complete darkness, so I pull out the flashlight and switch it on. The beam is weak, but it helps. "Étienne," I call again.

I keep calling as I move through the woods, but I get no response. I wonder if I should wait and see if he shows up, but it's probably not a good idea to hang around too close to the airfield, so I keep going. After about half an hour of stumbling through the trees, I arrive back at the farm.

Adelle is standing in the kitchen doorway. "Ah, my girl," she says. "Come. Hurry."

"Where's Étienne?" I ask.

"Hurry, hurry," Adelle repeats without answering my question. She waves me past her into the kitchen.

Étienne is sitting at the rough table. Across from him, dressed in a Royal Flying Corps uniform and with a crude bloodstained bandage around his head, sits the pilot who flew me across the front line last December.

"Good evening," he says with a smile. "I was passing and thought I'd drop in and say hello. It's lovely to see you again."

Chapter 13

Rescue—April 29, 1917

"What are you doing here?" I blurt out.

"His aircraft crashed in the trees," Étienne explains.

"Fritz got a couple of lucky shots in," says the pilot. "One caught my gunner, Sid, through the heart. Killed him, I'm afraid. I was fortunate—a bullet just grazed my thick skull. Knocked me out for a moment, though. Lucky for me I came to in time to haul the old bird over the trees, or else I'd be as dead as poor Sid right now. Managed to bring the plane down in a clearing."

"That's where I found him," Étienne adds.

"You shouldn't have brought him back here," Adelle says, wringing her hands. "When the Boches find the plane, they will come looking for him."

"I couldn't leave him to die like his companion," Étienne replies. "But you are correct, my dear. He cannot stay here."

"And neither can I," I say. "Someone saw me at the airfield." I hesitate. "And I'm the one who set the zeppelin on fire."

"It was you?" the pilot asks.

I nod. "With the flare gun that I was supposed to signal you with. I fired it at the man who discovered me. I missed him—"

"And hit the zeppelin," the pilot interrupts. "Well, it is a much bigger target. They'll give you a medal for that in London, but I doubt Fritz will be any happier with you than he will with me. I think we should both move on. But to where?"

We look at each other in silence for a moment and then an idea pops into my head.

"I know," I say.

"Where?" Étienne asks.

"It's probably better if you don't know," I tell him, "but we should leave soon. Do you have a spare bicycle?"

"I have one in the barn."

"Are you all right to travel?' I ask the pilot.

"Right as rain," he replies. "Well, bit of a headache, to be honest, but that shouldn't stop me from taking part in a cycling tour of your beautiful country."

Étienne heads to the barn to retrieve my bicycle and one for the pilot, while Adelle bustles around the kitchen collecting food for our journey. "I can get you some of Etienne's old clothes," she suggests.

"Thanks," the pilot says, "but best not to. If I'm to be captured, at least I won't be shot as a spy if I'm wearing uniform."

Adelle nods agreement and, half an hour after we met again, the pilot and I are cycling north through the darkness.

"Since we are cycling into the unknown together," the pilot says, drawing his bicycle next to mine, "we should be introduced. I'm Pilot Officer Albert Morris, at your service."

"My name's Manon Wouters," I say, but I don't really want to get into a conversation with Albert Morris. Part of my mind is still back at the airfield, and the rest is working out the route we must take and calculating if we have enough time to get to our destination before daylight. On top of that, I don't want to be distracted. I can barely make out the road in front of me, so I have to rely on hearing any danger ahead, and for that I need to concentrate.

"Where are we headed, Manon Wouters?" Albert asks.

"Somewhere that I hope is safe."

"Is it far?"

"It will take us most of the night," I say. "I think it's too dangerous for us to cycle side by side, especially with you still in your uniform. If we stumble on someone in the dark I might be able to talk my way out of it, but you won't. I think you should drop back."

"But if I'm too far back, I won't be able to see you if you turn or have to stop."

"I still have Étienne's flashlight. I'll tuck it under my arm so that it shines behind me. You drop back until you can just see the light and follow it. If the light goes out, get off the road and hide as fast as you can."

"All right," Albert says.

He drops back and I tuck the flashlight under my arm. It's a bit awkward to keep it in place, but it's impossible to go very fast in the dark in any case.

I'm quite pleased with my flashlight idea, but what I haven't told Albert is that if I do run into a German sentry, my chances of talking my way out of it, especially after what happened at the airfield, are virtually nil. If I run into trouble, Albert's on his own.

As we cycle along the tree-lined road, I wonder if I've made the right decision. The only refuge I could think of is Pieter's house in Maldegem. He has the space to hide Albert and seems to have the contacts to smuggle him across the border into neutral Holland. I hate to put Pieter in so much danger, but Albert couldn't stay with Étienne and Adelle. The Germans will sweep the surrounding countryside as soon as they find the crashed plane, and Albert would be shot or captured almost immediately. And of course I can't hide him in Damme with Florien and his friends around.

I don't have a choice. We have to keep going. At the very least, Pieter will have an idea where we can go. And if I'm honest with myself, I'm thrilled at this new adventure. Of course I'm scared, but I'm doing something real. I have destroyed a hated zeppelin and now I'm rescuing a crashed pilot. And I like Albert. With his cheerful and uncomplaining attitude, he reminds me of Alec. "Did you get the letter I wrote you in London?" I ask the Alec in the one-sided conversation in my head. "I wish I could have written more. Did you try to find out where I was? What are you doing now? Still digging holes in the ground?" I smile into the darkness.

We make good time, and as the half-moon rises, we stop and eat the food that Adelle provided. But Albert is having trouble keeping his eyes open and slumps against a tree. I check his head wound. The bandage is still in place, but the wound remains open and blood is trickling down his cheek. I clean him up as much as possible and retie the bandage more tightly.

"Thank you," Albert says when I've finished. "I'm lucky to have my own private nurse. I think I'm falling in love with you."

Albert's comment is meant in fun, but it makes me strangely angry. Alec's the only patient I want falling in love with me. "Don't be silly," I say, more harshly than I intend. "Everyone falls in love with their nurse. It doesn't mean anything."

"I'm grateful for your help, even if you don't love me back," Albert says with a smile. "Are you ready to tell me where we're going?"

"I have a friend, Pieter, who I think might be able to hide you until you can be smuggled across the border into Holland."

"Is it far?"

"Far enough that the Germans won't think of looking for you there."

Albert falls silent and his head slumps onto his chest. I wonder if he's fallen asleep, but then he says, "Perhaps I should just have surrendered."

Thinking that he's worried about the distance we have to travel, I say, "The moonlight will help us and we'll make better time from now on. Even if we stop for rests, we'll be at Pieter's well before dawn."

"Oh, I'll push on," Albert says, lifting his head. "Don't worry about me. But I'm getting a lot of people into trouble—Étienne, Adelle, you, and now your friend Pieter. Maybe you should just go on and

I'll wait here until a German shows up to capture me. I can say I stole the bicycle and got lost. The head wound will help my story, and life in a German prison camp can't be too bad."

"No!" I say, surprising myself with the firmness of my voice. "You must never give up. Yes, Étienne, Adelle, Pieter and I will be at risk, but we accept that. It is the price of the struggle to free our country from these invaders. If nobody is prepared to pay that price"—I think of Florien and my anger increases—"or if people collaborate with the Germans, we will never be free. Even if the Allies win the war and liberate Belgium, we cannot hold our heads up if we have done nothing. What will we tell our children after the war—that we sat back while others fought our battles for us?"

Albert has been staring at me throughout my rant. "But you're so young to be so bitter," he says. "And you're a girl."

"A girl!" I exclaim, my anger boiling over. "Are you so arrogant that you think a girl cannot be as intelligent, powerful or courageous as you? What do you do—fly around all day, dropping bombs on people? Let me tell you about a girl."

"I'm sorry. I didn't mean—" Albert begins, but I hold up my hand to silence him. I don't want to hear his apology.

"Gabrielle Petit was a nurse like me. Like me, she also became a spy. Through 1915, she created a network of couriers and passed on vital information about the German army to the Allies. In February last year, she was betrayed and captured. Despite torture, she wouldn't give the names of her fellow spies. On April 1 she was tied to a post and shot. She refused to wear a blindfold and stared straight at her executioners. Many of the soldiers on the firing squad closed their eyes and fired high. An officer had to administer the coup de grâce. Gabrielle's last words to her jailer were 'I will show you how a Belgian girl can die.' She had just turned twenty-three years old."

I stare hard at Albert, daring him to argue with me. But he just looks at me with his jaw hanging open.

"Well, then," he says eventually, "I think I'm very lucky to have met a girl like you, Manon Wouters. Shall we get back on the road?"

Still angry, I push my bicycle out of the trees and almost collide with a German soldier. He's even more surprised than I am and stumbles awkwardly. His uniform is unbuttoned at the neck and he's having difficulty standing straight. I realize that he is drunk and is probably trying to find his way back to camp after a night in a local bar.

His wandering gaze finally fixes on me and he blinks several times as he attempts to focus. A smile spreads across his unshaven face. "Fräulein," he slurs, stepping forward. My bicycle is between us, which makes it hard for him to reach me but also difficult for me to defend myself. I'm still wondering what to do when a shadow appears behind the soldier. There's a surprisingly loud thump, and the man crumples to the ground as if his bones have turned to water. Albert is standing over the body, clutching a large rock.

I drop my bicycle and bend over the fallen soldier, feeling his neck for a pulse. "He's alive," I say.

"Then we should finish him off," Albert replies, lifting the rock.

"No!" I step between the two soldiers.

"We don't want him to wake up and raise the alarm."

"I won't let you kill him," I say firmly. "He's roaring drunk. I doubt he'll remember anything when he comes around."

Albert stands and stares at me for a moment, and then tosses the rock into a ditch. "All right," he says, "but we should get him off the road."

Together we drag the man into the trees and prop him against a trunk. He's breathing regularly and I take time to make him as comfortable as possible.

"We need to go," Albert says urgently. "He may have mates on their way back from the bar, and we want to put as much distance as we can between us and him before he wakes up."

"Yes," I agree. "And thank you."

"Always happy to help a lady in distress," Albert says with a smile. When he sees the flash of anger on my face, he quickly adds, "Even one who can obviously look after herself."

Chapter 14

Betrayal—April 30, 1917

It's still dark when we arrive at Maldegem. Hiding our bicycles near the road, we approach Pieter's house cautiously, working our way through the trees at the edge of town. The first sign that something is wrong is the smell of burning. I tell Albert to wait and he sits gratefully at the foot of a tree. I move forward carefully, but even so, I almost fall over the remains of Pieter's shed. The burned wood is still warm, and so are the bodies of the dead pigeons scattered around the ruins. What's happened? Was it an accident, or something much worse?

I edge out of the trees and into Pieter's vegetable garden, where the moonlight is brighter, picking my way across to his house. I knock gently on the back door. There's no response. I try the handle. The door's unlocked, so I slip inside. I call out softly, "Pieter. Pieter?" But there's no reply. I feel my way carefully from room to room. The house is empty. What has happened? Has Pieter been arrested?

I grope my way to the front door. It's broken, hanging off its hinges. I slump down against the wall. Clearly someone's forced his way in, taken Pieter away and burned down the pigeon shed. I'm drained. I can't go on. The bombing raid, the zeppelin, cycling all night, the German soldier, and now this—I have nothing left. What if Pieter was betrayed? What if the whole organization's been betrayed? Maybe there are German soldiers waiting for me outside my house. All I want to do is sit here in the darkness and let the world happen. If the Germans find me, I don't care. It would be a relief, in fact—there would be no more stress, no more strain. I wouldn't have to think and make decisions anymore. My head slumps onto my chest. I'm so tired.

I jerk awake at the sound of the back door opening. "Pieter?" I ask.

Shuffling footsteps come closer. "No, it's me, Albert. Are you all right?"

"Pieter's gone," I say, hauling myself to my feet. "I think he's been arrested."

Albert stands beside me and puts a comforting arm around my shoulder. "Well, I guess you can't stay here. I'll wait until daylight so you have a chance to get far away—I could use a nap anyway—then I'll walk into town and surrender. I'll tell the stolen bicycle story and play up the head wound."

"No," I say, brought back to life by the idea of surrender. "We've come too far to give up. Remember all the things I said about being able to face our children after the war? Gabrielle Petit would never give up. Let them catch us if they can, but we'll keep fighting until the end."

Albert stares at me for a long moment. His eyes are red with exhaustion, his skin is ghostly pale and a thin stream of blood is once more trickling down his cheek.

"Manon Wouters," he says at last, "you are an extraordinary person. Let's give them a run for their money. Where shall we go?"

"South of my home, there's a deep wood on an old estate where my brother and I used to play as children. It's private land, but we knew the secret ways in. We used to take picnics and go far into the woods to build forts and pretend that we were explorers living in the wilderness. There's a ruined hut in there—I think it used to be the gamekeeper's place. It's just overgrown walls, but it will give you some shelter and no one will think of looking for you there.

You can hide and I will bring you clothes and food until I can contact someone to help." If there's anyone left to help, I think.

Albert smiles weakly. "Good idea, but I hope this estate isn't too far. I'm not sure I can last much longer."

"It's not far," I say as encouragingly as possible. "One last effort and then you can rest."

"Right you are," Albert says. "Let's get going."

~~~~~

By sunrise, Albert is safe in the gamekeeper's hut and gratefully asleep. He's under strict instructions not to move during the day and to wait for me to return with clothing and food. If I don't show up it means I can't, and Albert is to walk out of the woods and surrender to the first person he meets.

I'm leaning against a wall, peering out of the alley across the road from my house, trying to spot anything unusual. The house looks undisturbed and there are no German soldiers waiting to ambush me. I know I should watch for a while to make sure it's safe, but my legs feel so heavy that I'm not certain I can even make it the short distance across the road. If I collapse here from exhaustion, I'll be discovered as soon as anyone passes by.

I scan the street once more. There's no one around, so I take a deep breath, mumble a soft prayer that there are no soldiers waiting for me to show myself and stumble across the road using my bicycle for support.

With a sigh of relief, I drop the bicycle beside the door and enter the house. Mama is sitting at the kitchen table and jumps up as I come in.

"Where have you been?" she asks frantically. "I've been worried sick."

If I wasn't so drained of energy, both mental and physical, I could have thought of an explanation, but my mind's not working properly. "I had something to do," I say.

"What? What did you have to do that kept you out all night? Are you seeing a boy?"

"No, Mama. I'm not seeing a boy. There are things I have to do, but I'm too weary to talk about them now."

"Are you in danger?"

The answer's yes, but instead I say, "I'm all right, Mama. I'm safe. I'm just very tired. I'll explain everything later." I go over and give her what I hope is a reassuring hug. "I have to go to the hospital today, but I need to sleep a bit first."

"Is there anything I can do to help?"

I give her another hug. "Don't worry. Everything will be fine. Can you wake me in two hours?"

I head for my room and bump into Florien in the hall. "Back late," he says with a sneer.

I push past him into my room and collapse on the bed. My muscles unclench with gratitude. The last thing I remember thinking before Mama knocks on my door to wake me is that I have never been this comfortable in my entire life.

~~~~~

"I've made some bread and jam and a hot drink," Mama says when I am awake enough to grunt a reply to her.

"I'll be there in a minute," I reply. I haul my aching body off the bed, splash some cold water on my face from the bowl by the window and change into some clean clothes.

In the kitchen, I give Mama an abbreviated version of what I have been up to. I don't mention any specifics, and I certainly don't talk about the danger I've been in. I simply say that I'm collecting information, and that sometimes it means being out after curfew.

I suppose I expect Mama to respond with tears and beg me not to do anything dangerous, but she surprises me.

"I'm so proud of you," she says, giving me a huge hug. "Papa would be too."

"Do you think so?" I ask.

"Of course. When the Germans invaded, the roads were filled with people heading west. Papa and I talked about joining them and crossing into Holland, but he refused to leave. He said it would be running away, and he had never run away from a problem in his life. He said it was our responsibility to stay and make life as difficult as possible for the invaders."

"If I had known that was how he felt," I say, "I would never have left."

Mama smiles. "You were old enough to make your own decisions. Besides, you did help. You used your nursing skills to help the British soldiers. And now you're back, doing what Papa would have done."

A knot of emotion almost chokes me. I suddenly feel as if Papa is watching over me—as if, whatever I have to do, I will never have to do it alone. Papa will always be with me. Then a darker thought intrudes. "And Florien?"

Mama's smile vanishes. "Papa would have been disappointed in the path Florien has chosen, but don't be too harsh on your brother. He worshipped Papa. He took his death very hard. You didn't see it all after Papa died, but Florien sat in his room for days, not eating or sleeping. I heard him crying at all hours.

"He eventually came out, but he wasn't the same. There was a coldness in him that I had never seen before. When the Germans came to conscript him for work on the docks, he went without a murmur, even though several of his school friends went over the border into Holland. Then he fell in with that crowd of layabouts and began drinking. I've tried talking to him, but he just gets angry and storms out. It's as if he's a different person now."

"I know," I agree. "He's changed so much since I left. But I'll keep trying to talk to him. Maybe if I tell him how Papa felt about the Germans?"

"Please don't tell him that." Mama's pleading surprises me. "I tried to explain that to him once. It was the worst fight we ever had. I truly feared he would hit me in his anger, but he just walked out instead. I didn't see him for three days after that."

"All right, Mama, I won't say anything," I assure her. I look at the clock and gulp down the rest of my drink. "I have to go now. I'm already late for my shift at the hospital and I have information to pass on."

Mama nods. "Be careful," she says.

As I cycle along the canal bank, I think over the past couple of days. Spying has turned out to be much more complicated than I expected. I've photographed secret enemy airplanes, destroyed a zeppelin and rescued a British pilot. Three times I've almost been captured. If it weren't for Étienne and his cart, Albert and his rock, and my own flare gun, I wouldn't be here now.

To complicate things even more, Pieter has disappeared, and the path to send messages to the British has been destroyed. But I'm oddly happy. Now I'm doing what I do not just for Belgium but for Papa.

Chapter 15

An Idea—April 30, 1917

I'm halfway through my shift before I get a chance to talk to Amelie. We retreat to the supply room and speak quietly. She says nothing, only nodding occasionally, as I swiftly give her an outline of my adventure.

When I have finished, she says, "First the good news: Pieter is all right. A neighbour who works at the town office managed to get him a note telling him that the Germans were planning to arrest him. He got out the back door into the woods as they were breaking down the front door."

"Was he betrayed?"

"It looks like it. They certainly knew about the pigeons. But was it someone in the organization or neighbour with a grudge?" Amelie shrugs. "Enough people in Maldegem knew about Pieter's father's pigeons, and it wouldn't take a genius to work out what they could be used for. It was probably inevitable."

"I'm glad he got away," I say. "Where is he now?"

"He's hiding at my house."

"In Damme?"

Amelie nods. "But it's dangerous. One glimpse of him by my neighbours and word will get out to the guys who beat me up. He has to leave the country."

"Pieter has contacts for getting over the border, hasn't he?"

"Yes, but there's no way of knowing who to trust. Maybe it was one of them who betrayed him."

"What can we do?" I feel helpless and lonely without any contact to London and Major Macleod. "We need to get Albert out of the country as well. He can't live in the woods until the war's over."

"There may be a way we can contact London. Pieter told me that he has a backup method for contacting his father in Holland. He sends messages at precise times, and if one doesn't arrive, his father is to go and check a specific place where things can be thrown over the electric fence. Pieter missed sending a message last night, so his father will be checking every night for something thrown over the fence. My plan is to go there and get him a message telling him what happened to Pieter and asking him to contact London for instructions. I will tell them about Albert as well. Perhaps they can organize a boat to pick them up somewhere on the coast."

"That will take time to arrange," I point out.

"I know," Amelie agrees, "but we have no other choice. We must hide Pieter and Albert until something can be set up. Pieter can stay with me, but what about your airman?"

"I can't take him home. I can't trust Florien."

"Is he safe where you left him?"

"I think so," I reply. "Not comfortable, but probably safe. No one goes into those woods except hunters, and the Germans don't allow people to have weapons anymore. He'll probably be all right for a few days, provided the weather doesn't get too bad. I'll take him food."

"What about clothes? I can get some."

"As long as he doesn't go anywhere, he's better in his pilot's uniform. It's warm and if he does get captured he won't be shot as a spy. But when he leaves the woods, he'll need civilian clothes."

Amelie nods thoughtfully. "You did well," she says. "Let's hope we don't have to wait too long for an answer from London."

"Come on," I say. "We should get back to work."

Amelie puts a hand on my arm. "When Pieter came to my house last night, he brought the latest message from London. They want us to do something else."

"What?" My voice is so loud that Amelie glances nervously at the door. "Is there no rest? Don't they understand that we're risking our lives here?"

"You have a right to be angry," she says calmly. "You have risked your life more than most in the past few days. But I fear we live in a time when risk is normal."

"I'm sorry," I reply, calming down a bit. "I'm just tired. What is it they want us to do?"

Amelie hesitates long enough that I realize whatever she's about to say will not be easy. I feel a knot forming in my stomach at the thought of having to go back to Gontrode. Surely I won't get away with it a third time.

"They want us to get into the docks in Bruges and photograph the U-boat pens."

It takes me a moment to understand what Amelie has just said. "That's impossible," I reply. "I was successful at Gontrode only because of the size of the airfield and the lax security. Even with that, I was almost caught—twice. The Germans know the U-boat docks are a major target, and that's been proved by all the bombing raids over the past few weeks. The docks will be crawling with German soldiers and sailors. The security will be incredible. It won't just be a question of slipping through a hole in a wire fence and running across an open field."

I'm talking too much because I'm nervous. Amelie already knows everything I'm saying, but she listens patiently all the same. When I've finished, she says, "Everything you say is true, but we have to try. And the very size of the docks may help."

"How?"

"There are thousands of Belgian workers going in and out every day. It would be hard to spot one more."

"Do we have a contact among the workers?"

Amelie shakes her head. "I wish we had. That's why we were so hoping that you could persuade Florien to work with us. The Germans screen the workers very carefully, and every one has personalized identification."

"And they are all men?"

"Yes," Amelie answers. "The men are used for the heavy construction work. There are women who work at the canteen, but that's some distance from the docks themselves. It would be difficult for a woman to move between the two without attractive suspicion."

"How are we to do it, then?"

"I don't know," Amelie admits, "but we'll need to find a way."

I nod agreement. "Florien keeps a chart of the amount of shipping tonnage sunk each month. I go into his room and look at the chart when he's not home. It shows that U-boats sunk half a million tons in March alone, and his numbers show almost twice that this month."

"The British will starve," Amelie adds. "They have to stop the U-boats somehow, and it's much easier if they can destroy them before they get out to sea. That makes the lock gates at Zeebrugge and Ostend—as well as the dockyards here in Bruges—vital targets. But the lock gates are very small targets. It's much easier to bomb the docks and pens in Bruges."

"If the pens are as strong as we think, do the British have a bomb big enough to destroy them?"

"Maybe not destroy them," Amelie admits, "but the British have a new bomber plane that they think can carry bombs big enough to damage the U-boat pens, and for that they need information on exactly where the pens are and how they're built."

"When does London want the information?"

"Soon."

But I can think of no way of gaining access to the dockyard, and I can see another possible difficulty as well. "Without Pieter's pigeons and contacts, we don't have a secure route to pass our information to London. And we can't use anyone else in the network because we don't know if there's a traitor or not."

"I know. It all puts more pressure on us. I hope I can establish something with Pieter's father tonight, but however difficult it is, we have to try. If Britain starves, the war is lost."

All that Amelie has said weighs heavily on my mind as I return to work. Just when everything seems to be falling apart, we are given a task that appears impossible.

I'm still thinking about the problem when I walk into the ward and see Manfred sitting up in bed and smiling at me. I'm about to return the smile when I stop and stare, suddenly realizing why he looked vaguely familiar the first time I saw him. An insane idea takes root in my mind, and I turn and stride out of the ward.

I have to talk to Amelie.

Chapter 16

The Plan—April 30, 1917

It's mad," Pieter says.

"It's worse than mad," I say. "It's suicidal. But as Amelie says, we have to do something, and do we have a better plan?"

She and I are sitting at her kitchen table, telling Pieter the plan we came up with as we cycled back from Bruges after work.

He's silent for a long time, gazing at Amelie and me in turn. "Okay," he says eventually. "I accept that getting Manon into the docks as a nurse during an air raid might work, but—"

I interrupt before he can begin to list his objections. "It all has to work. Me getting in is not enough. I can't just walk around taking photographs in the middle of an air raid. I have to have a reason to be near the U-boat pens."

"And she has to have a way to get out of the docks afterward," Amelie adds. "The second part of the plan provides those things."

We both stare at Pieter.

"Several things have to happen before we can go ahead," he says. Amelie and I nod enthusiastically. At least he's now recognizing the possibility. "Everyone has to agree." We nod again. "The British may not want to send their new bombers on an air raid before we give them the information they're asking for."

"On the other hand," Amelie says, "if we're there when the raid happens, we can report on the damage done and they can use that information to make the next raid even better."

"I'll put that in the message," Pieter says, nodding. "They'll also have to tell us when the raid is going to be and set up a meeting place somewhere afterward. It will all take a lot of very precise planning."

"We can do that," I say.

"All right," Pieter agrees, and Amelie and I smile at each other. "But if the British say no for any reason, we drop the whole idea. Understood?"

"Understood," Amelie and I say together.

Pieter looks at me. "Now I need to write the message for Amelie to take to my father, and you need to go and feed your hidden pilot."

~~~~~

"This is the best soup I've ever tasted," Albert says appreciatively. He must be either very hungry or very polite because the soup is only a weak broth made from boiling a few turnips, cabbage and potatoes. But he's not polite enough to compliment the bread, which is gray and gritty.

We're sitting against the tallest of the ruined walls of the old gamekeeper's hut, Étienne's torch providing a pale illumination. It was sunny and warm today, but the temperature dropped rapidly when the sun went down and here in the midst of the woods, there's a distinct chill in the air. "Were you warm enough today?" I ask.

"Toasty," Albert replies. "Remember, I'm wearing a suit that keeps me from freezing ten thousand feet up in the air. Got a visitor, though."

"What?" I ask. "Someone knows you're here?"

Albert laughs. "Don't worry, he won't tell anyone. There I was comfy and having a lovely dream about being back home when a snuffling noise woke me up and I came face to face with this ugly, hairy pig with tusks sticking out of his mouth. I don't know who got the bigger fright, but he left on the double."

"A wild boar," I say, relaxing. "Nobody's allowed to hunt them anymore, so there are a lot roaming about in the woods. How's your head?"

"A bit sore but healing nicely. I'll be right as rain by the time I get home."

"Let me have a look," I say, ignoring Albert's comment about going home. I fuss over his wound, cleaning it and tying a fresh bandage in place. While I work, I examine him closely. When I've finished, I sit back and stare at him.

"What?" he asks. "You look like a lioness that's just found a wounded antelope."

"You look like someone I know."

"I don't think I have any relatives hereabouts," Albert says, smiling. "At least none that I know of."

"He's a German naval officer," I explain.

Albert's smile is replaced by a frown. "I don't understand. How do you know a German naval officer?"

"He's a patient at the hospital where I work. He has a head wound from a bombing raid on the docks in Bruges."

Albert takes another drink of soup without taking his eyes off me. "And..." he says.

"You know that I'm a spy?"

"You fly into Belgium in the middle of the night and then go merrily about blowing up zeppelins and helping lost British flyers. I'm not smart, but I worked out that you weren't here on holiday."

I smile despite my nervousness. But before I can say anything, Albert goes on.

"By the way you're taking so long to get to the point, I'm guessing that you're going to ask me to do something I won't be keen on, and that the something is related to my lost twin, the German naval officer?" Albert raises his eyebrows questioningly.

"You're right," I say, "but first I have to tell you a story."

Albert sips his soup, chews his bread and listens intently as I tell him about the submarine pens, the bombing of the Bruges dockyard, Florien's charts of the amount of damage done by the U-boats and the request for information from London.

"I've heard about those new bombers," he says when I've finished. "Handley Pages, they are—as big as the Gothas, apparently. If anything can get at those U-boats, it will be them." He tilts his head slightly to the side. "And now comes the part I'm not going to like."

"The docks are big," I explain. "There's a lot of work going on, and the Germans cover most of it with camouflage netting. No one really knows what the U-boat pens look like. There is so much anti-aircraft fire during a raid that no one can fly low enough for a good look. Observation flights and air photographs aren't much use."

"Hence the need for someone to go in on the ground."

"Exactly," I say. "The problem is that the security's very tight, so someone needs identification to get in. I could probably manage it during an air raid because I'm a nurse, but if I start wandering around looking at things instead of tending to the wounded, the Germans will become very suspicious very fast."

"I'm beginning to see where this is going, and I'm guessing that your German officer is about the same size as me."

"With his uniform, his identification and a bandage around your head, you could pass for him."

"Until I open my mouth."

"And that's where the head wound comes in. In the middle of a bombing raid, no one will question a wounded officer. Once you're inside, you can go where you want."

"Accompanied by my very own private nurse."

"Exactly. Then when we're finished, we walk out to the hospital to have that nasty head wound treated. Except a plane or a launch comes to pick you up and take you—and the photographs and other information—back to London instead."

Albert chews his upper lip thoughtfully. "It's a pretty harebrained scheme," he says at last. "I've only just heard about it and already I can think of a dozen things that could go horribly sideways—not least of which is a British flying officer being discovered in a secret German U-boat base wearing a stolen naval uniform."

"It's your decision," I say. "Nobody's ordering you."

"Just so I'm clear, you want me—a British pilot who speaks not a word of German—to impersonate a German officer, sneak into a high-security dockyard and wander round with a Belgian spy so she can take photographs?"

"You forgot the bit about there being an air raid in progress."

"Of course. Silly of me. Well, that clinches it, then." He grins. "How can I possibly refuse?"

"Are you sure?"

"No," Albert says. "Every time I go up in that old stringbag F.E.2b to drop bombs over enemy lines, I wish I was back at home. Every time I frantically dodge enemies who fly faster, more deadly planes, I wonder about my sanity. Every time I see an empty chair at the mess table because some new kid has gone down in a flaming death trap, I wonder if I'll be next. No, I'm not sure, but that's not the point. The point is it has to be done, and I'm the lucky bloke who looks like the German officer. So when do we do this?"

I spontaneously lean forward and kiss Albert on the cheek.

"That's a pleasant bonus," he says with a smile. "Promise me another kiss at the end and I'll learn German."

"A few words might not be a bad idea," I suggest. "Are you all right staying here for a few more days?"

"Now that the boar and I have established who's boss, I think I'll be fine. When will our adventure begin?"

"That depends on London. The message is going out tonight and it stresses the urgency. If our German officer recovers and goes back on duty or is sent home on leave, the whole plan falls apart. I'll bring food every night. Is there anything else you need?"

"Something to read would be good."

"I have the perfect book. I'll bring it tonight."

"I'll look forward to it."

I cycle back home deep in thought. I like Albert—he jokes and makes light of everything, even though he knows this plan might easily lead to disaster. A part of me hopes that London will squash the whole idea. Then we can concentrate on getting Albert over the border, and I can get back to the more mundane task of collecting information from wounded sailors. It's a comforting idea, but deep down I know it won't happen. I came here to make a difference, and making a difference is risky. There's no turning back. I have to finish the dangerous game I've begun.

Chapter 17

The Answer—May 11, 1917

It's been almost two weeks since Amelie passed our urgent message over the wire to Pieter's father. Every night she has returned to see if there's a reply. Every morning I've waited with increasing nervousness to know what news she has. This morning, as soon as I see her cycling towards me, hair flying in the wind and an intense look on her face, I know she's had a response.

"It's on for May 12," she says as soon as we are on the canal path outside town.

"That's tomorrow night!" I exclaim in horror. "There's not enough time. That gives us only thirty-six hours to get the uniform for Albert, get into position, and plan where we meet and what we do inside the dockyard."

"Less."

"What do you mean?" I'm so upset that I'm having trouble keeping my bike from wobbling off the path into the canal.

"They're planning to coordinate the bombing raid on Bruges with a major raid on Zeebrugge. They hope to destroy the lock with shelling from ships offshore, and the shelling is scheduled to begin at three o'clock tomorrow morning. The bombing of the Bruges docks will begin at three thirty."

I do a quick calculation in my head. "That's less than twenty hours away. Couldn't they have given us more warning?"

"I don't think so. We're just piece of the puzzle and the shelling of Zeebrugge depends on cloud cover, wind direction, tides and many other factors we can't even guess at. Everything has to be arranged to give the navy the best chance of success, and we have to fit in. There's no choice."

We cycle in silence for a while. Now that the shock is wearing off, my mind begins to work. "I have to steal Manfred's uniform and identification today. It will be difficult to do it in broad daylight, not to mention bring it back on my bicycle, but I'll manage somehow. I can take the uniform to Albert after sunset, but he'll have to come up to Bruges in the uniform, which increases the chance of being caught. I need a coat for him. I'll borrow Florien's—that should hide the uniform in the dark. And Albert'll need to shave. I'll take Florien's razor down to him as well."

My mind is racing, coming up with solutions almost before I've thought of the problem. "Albert and I won't have time to organize a rendezvous inside. Maybe we can just go through the main gate together. But how do we explain that in the middle of the night?"

"If you wait until the bombing starts, you can say he was injured outside by a stray bomb and you're bringing him in," Amelie suggests. "With the raid going on, I doubt anyone will pay too much attention."

"That might work. And as long as we go out a different gate after, I can say we're going to the hospital. Are there any plans for getting Albert and the information out of the country?"

"Pieter's been working on that. He's found a suitable field north of town. A plane will land there before dawn to pick up Albert and you."

"Me! Why me?"

"Two reasons. They want a more detailed report on the bombing at Gontrode, and you'll have to describe the U-boat pens at Bruges."

"Albert can do that, probably better than me. He's got a military background."

Amelie brakes to a stop and I pull up beside her. She hands me a small package. "This is new film for your camera."

"Why? It will be night when I'm in the dockyard." I have so many questions, and I feel like I'm not getting many answers.

"It will be getting close to dawn. If we're lucky, the moon and the fires from the bombing raid will provide just enough light for a photograph. It's an outside chance, and in any case, your description will still be more important and detailed than a fuzzy picture or two."

"I still don't see why Albert can't give as good a description as I can."

Amelie looks at me. "I asked them to fly you to London."

"What? Why?" I feel betrayed by my friend.

"I think it would be good if you went," Amelie explains. "You've done magnificent work in a short time, but it will be dangerous for you after tomorrow. They'll find out that Manfred's uniform was stolen, and that someone impersonating him went into the docks during the raid. When they find out that he was accompanied by a nurse, they'll put two and two together and come looking for you. You'll have to go into hiding, and then you'll be no use as a spy. But right now, we can't worry about any of that. We have to focus on our task if it's to have any chance of success."

I don't like it, but I know Amelie's right. It will be very dangerous for me after tomorrow. It makes sense to get me out, but I don't want to go. I really feel that I have been doing something worthwhile, and despite the fear I've felt, there has been a thrill as well—a thrill I never got working in a hospital and tending patients. On the other hand, if I'm back in London, I might be able to find Alec. I find myself grinning stupidly at the thought of meeting him again, but I push my emotions down. I mustn't let my feelings get in the way of my work, especially now. We have to concentrate all our energies on the next twenty hours if we are to complete our tasks—and survive.

"There's one more thing," Amelie says, interrupting my thoughts, "and it's bad news, I'm afraid. Étienne has been arrested."

"No!" I exclaim.

"The Germans arrested several farmers from around the airfield. They think the saboteur who was spotted the night of the raid must have had help, and they are determined to find out from whom."

"Étienne won't say anything."

"I'm sure he won't, but we have no idea what the other farmers might know. And there's more. The drunk soldier can't remember anything about who attacked him, but the Germans have taken hostages from the village he was drinking in. They suspect that he was attacked by the British flyer who crashed near the airfield, and that he might have been helped by the saboteur. So, you see, the Germans are beginning to piece things together. The search is moving north, and that places you in even more danger. One more reason why you need to get on that plane tomorrow."

"Has Pieter worked out who betrayed him?" I ask.

"Not for certain, but he's fairly sure it's someone in Maldegem that he's been arguing with."

"So it was a neighbour with a grudge. The network's not been compromised."

"It looks that way."

"At least that's good news."

We cycle in silence the rest of the way into Bruges. I'm scared, but I've done enough to know that the hours before the real danger begins are the worst. It's a time when the mind obsessively reviews every possible way things can go wrong and the dozens of decisions that might have to be made. Once the action begins, the decisions become simple and immediate and I become oddly calm. To calm myself now, I begin to plan how I will go about finding Alec as soon as I get to London.

~~~~~

"I'm going home."

The first words Manfred says to me when I enter the ward send a chill down my spine. "When?" I manage to choke out.

"This afternoon," Manfred says happily. "I have my rail pass already."

"But you're still having nightmares."

"Yes," Manfred agrees, "but my physical injuries are healing well, and I am told there's a doctor in Mannheim who is working with soldiers who have exactly what is troubling me. He will make me better. It's wonderful news, is it not? Of course I shall miss you dreadfully."

I nod and force a smile. The whole plan is falling apart before it's even begun. I have to stop him leaving. So much depends on Albert being able to move around freely inside the dockyard.

"You look sad," Manfred says. "Are you not happy for me?"

"I am," I lie, "but I will miss you very much."

"Perhaps"—he offers a sly grin—"we can go somewhere and say good-bye...properly."

My first reaction is anger. I know what he's suggesting. Nursing crude soldiers and sailors—British and German—has taught me to handle vulgar propositions, but I had thought Manfred was different, more like Alec.

"What do you say?" he asks, holding out a hand.

I look at his smiling face and see it very differently than before. It's no longer the friendly expression of a wounded boy, but the leer of a man who just wants to get what he can—an enemy. An idea begins to form. I smile back at Manfred.

"There's a storeroom downstairs," I say in what I hope sounds like an eager voice.

Manfred's smile broadens and he slips out of bed to stand beside me. He's dressed in the coarse blue outfit that all the patients are given as soon as they're able to move about a bit. He takes my hand. "Let's go," he says.

I pretend to be helping Manfred as we walk down the ward. He has his arm around my shoulder and he's squeezing me too close to him. The corridor outside is empty and we head for the flight of stairs at the end. At the top of the stairs, Manfred pulls me round and tries to kiss me. Anger surges and I push him away. He teeters for a moment on the top step, his arms waving, and then, with a shout, he's gone, a ragged bundle of limbs tumbling down the concrete stairs to the landing below.

I'm still looking down in shock when Amelie appears behind me.

"What happened?" she asks. "I heard a shout."

"He fell," I say.

She pushes past me and down the stairs. I follow in a daze. Manfred's lying on the landing. I know he's dead even before Amelie checks for a pulse. His head is bent at an impossible angle.

"His neck's broken," she announces, looking round nervously. "What happened?"

"He was to leave for home this afternoon," I say. "I only intended to trip him when he was a couple of steps from the bottom—so that he would injure himself enough to be kept here for a few more days—but he tried to kiss me. I got angry and pushed him away, and he fell from the top."

"Go and get the doctor," Amelie orders. "Not that he'll be able to do anything." I turn to go up the stairs, but she holds me back. "This might work out in our favour, Manon. When someone dies, we pack up their belongings to take them to the German authorities. If you are the one to do that, you can walk out of the hospital with his uniform bundled under your arm."

I nod. "I didn't mean to kill him," I say, staring at the crumpled body. "I just...he wanted to..." I don't know what I'm trying to say. I've just killed someone, yet it all seems so unreal.

"It was an accident," Amelie says. "You had to try to stop him going away today. You didn't mean to kill him, but now that he's dead, we have to go on with the plan. Okay?"

I nod again and head up the stairs to find the doctor. Guilt is beginning to eat at me. Perhaps I'd killed other men when I set the zeppelin on fire, but I knew Manfred. He wasn't the charming young innocent I thought him to be, but he didn't deserve to die because of that. I didn't mean to kill him, but I had intended to injure him badly enough to keep him in hospital.

What really makes me feel guilty, though, is that a part of me is glad Manfred's dead. It makes the job I have to do easier. Does that make me a monster? I don't know and I can't dwell on it now. As Amelie said, we need to focus on the task at hand. Self-doubt will have to wait until later.

Chapter 18

Preparation—May 11-12, 1917

The bicycle ride home is a nightmare. Manfred's uniform, wrapped in brown paper and tied with string, lies like an accusation in my pannier. I cannot help remembering how excited he had been only that morning at the prospect of being sent away from the war. Had his family already been sent a letter announcing his imminent arrival? Instead of being on a train heading home, he's lying in the cold morgue at the hospital—and it's my fault.

I try to push the bleak thoughts from my mind, but I cannot. I had thought of spying as a way of stopping the war, of freeing my country, of reducing the number of mutilated soldiers sent to the hospitals where I worked. I had thought I would be the only one in danger, but it's not like that. This war seems to have a life of its own. It turns everyone it touches into a killer or a corpse.

I'm in a miserable mood as I park my bicycle beside the front door, but I'm determined to go through with what I have to do tonight. I pick up the package and go into the kitchen—only to find Florien sitting at the table with Mama.

"Shouldn't you be at work?" I say.

"Nice welcome," he says sarcastically. "More U-boats are on the way, so we have to work harder. I've been put on the night shift."

"Tonight?"

"That's when the night shift is," Florien answers harshly. In the last month, he's been working too hard and drinking too much. He's lost weight and looks pale. It has always been difficult to talk to him, but recently his only responses are curt and sarcastic. Even his crowing about the success of the U-boat campaign lacks the enthusiasm and conviction of before.

"I've been trying to persuade Florien to stop working at the docks," Mama says. "With all the air raids, it's getting very dangerous."

"Trying to persuade me to run away, more like," Florien sneers. "What do you want me to do—go and live in the forests like an animal? I'm not a coward."

"No one's calling you a coward," I say. "Mama's only worried about your safety."

"I can look after myself," he says scornfully, jumping up from the table. "I don't need advice from either of you. I have to go to work now." He storms out, slamming the door behind him.

Mama looks on the verge of tears. "I don't know what to do with him. I'm so worried."

I put my arm around Mama's shoulder. I want to put on a pot of tea and comfort her, but it's already getting dark outside and I have a busy night ahead of me.

"I'm sure Florien will be all right, Mama. Besides, he does have a point. If he stops going to work, the Germans will come looking for him and he'll have to go into hiding."

"I know," she says with a sigh. "I can't help worrying about him, though." She falls silent and stares at the tabletop.

"I have to go out tonight," I say.

Mama looks up at me. "I worry about you as well."

"I'll be fine," I say with a cheerfulness I don't feel. "I'm always careful."

Mama nods distractedly, and I go and get Florien's coat and razor. I eat a bowl of soup and some bread, then prepare some for Albert.

By the time I'm done, it's dark. I hug Mama, tell her again not to worry and set off.

~~~~~

"It's on for tonight."

"*Das ist gut. Ich bin bereit*," Albert replies, telling me he's ready.

"Your accent is dreadful," I say with a smile.

He exaggerates a look of misery. "I thought it was quite good for someone from a suburb of Munich."

"Yes, if he had grown up in London."

"Well, Champion likes my accent," he counters, using his nickname for the wild boar, which has returned several times. "Anyway, in the middle of an air raid I don't think anyone's going to be asking where I come from. It was a good idea to bring that old school textbook for me to learn from. I've had precious little else to do over the past days."

"You've learned a lot of useful phrases. That will help."

"*Danke, Fräulein.*"

"After you've eaten, you need to shave and get into the uniform. I'll bandage your head to hide some of your face, and then we can run over what you might have to say when we get to the dockyard gate. I'm hoping I can do all the talking, but it's best to be prepared."

"Yes, sir," Albert says.

The uniform fits well enough and the tears and bloodstains along the right arm add to the effect. In the beam of Étienne's flashlight, I explain Manfred's identification card to Albert and we spend some time polishing German phrases that might be useful.

"You look the part," I say, examining our handiwork. I get a lump in my throat as I think about Manfred, but I push the memory away. "I think you'll be a great actor."

"Charlie Chaplin's a great actor, but it's not my job to make the Germans laugh." Albert examines the bloodstains around the tears in the uniform. "These stains look awfully old."

"No one will notice in all the chaos," I say.

"We're relying on a lot not being noticed in this air raid," he points out. For a minute he stares at his arm, then he pulls out a small pocketknife and slashes the soft flesh over the ball of his left thumb. Blood, gleaming in the flashlight beam, wells up and forms a pool in his palm. "Spread this around a bit," he says, holding his hand out.

I'm shocked, but I do as he says, dipping my fingers and smearing the new blood over the old stains. Albert moves his thumb to keep the flow going. Eventually, we've made the wounds on his arm and the bandage on his head look much more convincing.

"Any bandage left over?" Albert asks. "I'd hate to bleed to death before I get to be a hero."

"That was brave," I say, attending to the cut on his hand.

"It was cowardly," he says with a grin. "I'm more afraid of being found out as a bad actor than of a tiny cut."

I finish work and we run over the plan one last time. "The shelling of Zeebrugge begins at three in the morning," I say "The air raid on the Bruges dockyard starts a half an hour after that. We'll wait until four o'clock—enough time for it to be plausible that you have been wounded in the raid—and then we'll go in. We have to leave by four forty-five and head north on the road to the village of Koolkerke. The plane will land on a field beside the road just before dawn, around five. It won't wait long."

"Got it," Albert says. He glances at his pocket watch. "It's after midnight. Should we be going?"

I nod. "We'll be all right on the open road, but we'll need to be very careful going through Bruges and that will be slow. The raid won't have started, so there will be nothing to distract the Germans."

We take a long route into Bruges, skirting the eastern edge of the town and then heading in along the canal I travel every day from Damme. As usual, I go first, to give Albert the chance to hide if there's trouble.

The moon, three-quarters full, rises in mostly clear sky shortly after we have left the woods, giving us enough light to navigate by, but exposing us to prying eyes. Despite this, we arrive at the outskirts of Bruges without incident. We dump the bicycles and work our way through the dark, empty street. We keep to alleys and shadowy courtyards, stopping often to examine any open space. At one point, we have to hide in an archway, huddled in the darkest corner, while a half dozen singing, drunken sailors stagger back to their billets.

At last we're in an alley across the road from the main gate into the dockyard. There is a high barbed-wire fence with broad double gates. Two guards are smoking outside a small hut.

"What time is it?" I whisper to Albert.

He squints at his pocket watch. "Quarter to three."

"Perfect. Let's move back to a safer spot. We'll have no trouble hearing the guns at Zeebrugge."

We move back and find a deep archway where someone will have to stumble over us to discover us. We wait...and wait.

By three thirty, Albert is moving into the moonlight every few minutes to check his watch. We've heard the occasional distant drone of aircraft but not a single sound of gunfire from Zeebrugge.

"What's happened?" Albert asks. "Has something gone wrong?"

"I don't know," I say, wondering what we will do if the raid has been cancelled and there is no bombing of the docks. Will the plane still arrive to pick us up?

At 3:45, we finally hear a distant drone. Searchlights begin to scan the sky. The sound of the approaching planes grows and anti-aircraft guns open up. At 3:55, the first bomb falls with a thunderous crash.

Chapter 19

The Raid—May 12, 1917

I don't know what happened at Zeebrugge," Albert says, "but we need to see what's happening here. Come on." He leads the way back into the alley and down to the corner where we can see the dockyard.

It's the raid on Gontrode magnified by ten, a medieval vision of hell. The intense beams of a dozen searchlights knife upward, sweeping back and forth as if trying to scour the bombers from the sky. Vivid explosions—red, green and white—blossom everywhere, illuminating the puffy black clouds left from previous detonations. It's hard to believe that any plane can survive in this sky, but they do. Swept by the moving searchlights—and occasionally trapped in a cone of two or three lights—are the new Handley Page twin-engined bombers.

Tiny planes dart between the lights and the bombers, but I can't tell whether they are German or British Certainly, the bombers are doing their job. The ground is shaking from explosions within the dockyards and the orange glow of raging fires is reflected in the growing clouds of smoke. An explosion erupts to our right, and pieces of shrapnel and masonry scatter along the cobbled street in front of us.

"This is our chance," Albert says, stepping away from the wall and taking off Florien's coat. "Help me across the road."

He drapes his left arm around my shoulder, I grab him around the waist, and we set off at a staggering, stumbling run across the road. The dockyard gates are open and figures are running in and out.

A guard with a rifle steps forward and asks, "Where are you going?"

"This officer was wounded by a bomb," I say. "He needs urgent attention."

The guard stares hard at Albert, who is doing a wonderful job of looking dazed and babbling unconnected German words. The guard seems satisfied and doesn't even ask for our identification. "The aid station is that way," he says, pointing to the right. "Be careful."

"Thank you."

Albert and I stumble off in the direction indicated. As soon as we're out of sight of the gate, he straightens and says, "Well, we're in. I hope the rest of the night goes as well."

As if to deny his hope, the building directly in front of us explodes and collapses in a pile of rubble. We change direction and race between two long warehouses, giving up all pretence of Albert being wounded. From what I saw of the docks before the war and with snippets of information that Florien has let slip, I have a vague map of the area in my head. The trouble is that it bares little relation to what we are moving through. Everything seems to be in motion, as if we're trapped in a spinning kaleidoscope of sound, vibrations and colour. I'm completely lost, but we have to go on.

We burst out into an open square where an anti-aircraft gun is hurling shells into the sky. Brass cartridge cases clang into the cobbles and skitter past our running feet, but the gun crew pays us no attention. In the next alley we enter, there's a destroyed water wagon, the dead horses still in harness and the driver on the ground beside them.

We run for what seems like an age, changing direction to avoid explosions and German gun emplacements. Sailors and Belgian civilians run all around us or cower against walls. Everyone is too wrapped up in their own work or fear to pay us any attention. Eventually, we slide around a corner and almost fall into a wide expanse of black water.

I know that the Bruges dockyard consists of four long tongues of water that stick out from the end of the major canal that runs to the sea at Zeebrugge. I have no idea which tongue we are looking at, however, as it looks nothing like the peaceful commercial dock I remember from before the war. Destroyers and torpedo boats are moored wherever there is space. Most of the dock to our left is taken up by what look like several cavernous pens. There's a reinforced concrete roof supported by rows of squat pillars. I see what must be the noses of a number of U-boats sticking out of the darkness of the pens. Any open space left is occupied by either a searchlight or an anti-aircraft battery.

To our right, a long concrete and metal roof covers the dock and overhangs the water. It's impossible to see what it covers because the whole structure is draped in green-and-brown camouflage netting. I count the pens on the left—four, but others are under construction beside them. I count the destroyers and smaller ships —three and fifteen, respectively. I count the thundering anti-aircraft batteries around the dock—thirteen. I count the searchlights—four.

I try to fix the scene in my mind: the docked ships, the running figures, the blazing guns, the exploding bombs. I take the camera out, set as long an exposure as I can and snap several pictures. I have no idea if any of them will come out, but I hope the moonlight, the searchlights, the glow of the nearby fires, and the flashes of the guns and bombs will create enough light to record something of use to London.

I work efficiently and without fear. It's as if I am separate from all the chaos around me, a detached observer. Even when a hot piece of metal falls painfully on my shoulder, I merely brush it off and continue photographing.

"What's under there?" Albert says pointing at the camouflage netting. He has to shout to make himself heard above the noise of the raid.

"Let's go and see," I say without hesitation.

We've taken only a couple of steps when a bomb explodes on the roof of the overhang, hurling several pieces of concrete into the water and shredding a long section of netting. Almost immediately, dozens of civilian workers who must have been sheltering under the overhang stream out. Albert and I push through them and haul a section of netting aside.

My heart leaps as I take in the scene before us. All my training as a spy and my desire to make a difference in the war effort has led to this moment. This is the heart of the dockyard and the centre of the attempt to starve Britain into submission.

Powerful lights hang from the roof to allow for nighttime work. Several are broken and others flicker uncertainly, but enough are working to let us see the sleek, dark shapes of twenty U-boats tied up beside the dock. They look like lurking, malignant sea monsters, their narrow decks only just breaking the black surface of the water. One even has red, staring eyes painted on the curved bow.

I hear Albert gasp beside me. A bomb explodes nearby, more lights flicker and small pieces of concrete drop around us. Workers are still streaming up from the depths of the dock. I take more photographs as surreptitiously as possible.

"Manon? What are you doing here?"

My heart leaps into my throat as I turn to see Florien coming toward us. He stares at me and then notices Albert in his bloodstained officer's uniform. His brow furrows in puzzlement.

"Are you wounded, sir?" he asks.

"Yes," Albert replies in his heavily accented German. "It was a bomb."

Florien continues to look confused. "Why are you here?" he asks turning his gaze back on me. "In the middle of an air raid?"

Albert steps forward, but his shaky command of German deserts him and he looks over at me helplessly.

Realization slowly dawns on Florien's face. "You're not a German officer," he says. He turns to me, eyes wide in shock. "You're a spy, like that woman at the hospital."

"Amelie," I say. "That's her name. You beat her up."

"I didn't," Florien says defensively.

"You didn't help her when your friends beat her," I say. "That amounts to the same thing."

"I told them to stop, but they wouldn't listen." His voice takes on a pleading tone. "Anyway, she's a spy."

"Yes, like me," I say angrily. "And not a spy—a patriot. Amelie is risking death for her country and what she believes in. What are you doing, bowing and scraping to the enemy?" In the midst of the bombing, I'm letting what I've long wanted to say to Florien flood out. "You would see us all enslaved rather than stand up for what is right. You want to let the Germans take everything good and worthwhile from us and break up our country."

"The Germans are going to win the war," Florien says weakly.

"Look!" I order, sweeping my arm around to encompass the bombers in the air and the explosions on the ground nearby. "Your precious U-boats don't stand a chance, and with America in the war, Germany is doomed. It won't be this year, but they cannot win. Just as those thugs you call friends won't achieve anything by beating up a defenceless woman."

"You ran away and deserted me," Florien says, his old anger flashing back. "Those thugs, as you call them, were the only friends I had. Mama was a wreck, you were gone and Papa..."

He sags as if he's been deflated and his gaze slides to the ground at his feet. Awareness of the world around me returns. The flow of people out of the U-boat pen has slowed and the bombing has almost stopped.

Albert is watching us, looking worried. "We have to go," he says urgently.

"What about Papa?" I ask Florien.

My brother looks up, tears glistening in the flickering firelight. He opens his mouth to say something, but a harsh voice interrupts.

"What is going on here?"

I spin round to see a German officer approaching. He's holding a pistol casually in his right hand.

"You shouldn't be here. This area is restricted."

Albert steps forward. "We came here in the bombing...safety," he says in awkward German, waving vaguely at the roof.

"He was wounded by a bomb," I say. "In the head. I brought him here for safety. I'll take him to the hospital now."

"And you?" The officer directs his pistol at Florien.

"I was on the night shift in here," Florien explains. "I was coming out after the bomb hit when I saw my sister." He nods toward me.

The officer stares hard at each of us in turn. "And why," he says, raising his pistol and pointing it at me, "would a nurse helping a wounded officer be carrying a camera?"

I almost collapse as I realize I still have the camera dangling from my left hand.

"I think maybe you are spying on us," the officer says. "Take that silly bandage off your head, please," he asks, swinging the gun round to point at Albert. Albert hesitates, although it's obvious from his gestures what the officer means. "I can shoot this young lady if you do not do as you are told."

Albert unwraps the bandage to show the almost healed wound from the raid on Gontrode.

"You heal very quickly," the officer says.

"She has nothing to do with it," Albert replies in English. "The camera is mine. I forced her to bring me in here. Don't shoot her."

"Very noble," the officer replies in broken English. "But I have no intention of shooting her. She probably has a wealth of useful information in that pretty head. You, on the other hand, are posing as a German officer. I will happily shoot you."

"No!" I yell, launching myself at the German. I intend to grab the gun, but the officer swings his arm back and the pistol catches me a stinging blow on the temple, knocking me to the ground.

I'm vaguely aware of a figure jumping over me and the sounds of a scuffle followed by a gunshot. There's some shouting, more scuffling and a second gunshot, then Albert is leaning over me.

"Are you all right?" he asks.

"Dizzy," I say, blinking my eyes and swallowing hard. "What happened?"

Albert helps me sit up. "You have to focus. Your brother attacked the German officer. He's wounded. He needs help."

At first, I think Albert means the German officer, but I look around to see Florien sitting on the dock with his right hand clutched over his chest. Dark blood is oozing between his fingers.

"Florien." I crawl over to my brother. The German officer is lying beside him, his eyes staring sightlessly at the sky.

Florien's breathing is shallow and there's a lot of blood on his overalls. "The gun went off," he says.

"Keep still. We'll get you to the hospital."

"I'm tired," Florien says, leaning against me.

I cradle his head on my lap. "You have to get up," I urge, tears running down my cheeks. "We have go to the hospital."

But Florien makes no attempt to move.

"You were very brave," I say. "You stopped that German shooting us."

"Where is he?" Florien asks.

"I took his gun and shot him," Albert explains.

Florien nods. "I couldn't allow him to hurt my big sister," he says with a smile. Suddenly, he's my little brother, being the knight in shining armour in the games we used to play in the forest. He coughs, a deep, gurgling sound. "There's something I have to tell you," he says when the fit passes.

"You can tell me later," I say through my tears. "Just rest now."

Florien shakes his head weakly. "I have to tell you now. It's important." Another cough rattles his body and a grimace crosses his face. "I killed Papa."

"No, you didn't," I say. "The Germans killed Papa."

"When the Germans first came to our town, everyone was so unhappy. I wanted to do something to make them go home."

He closes his eyes and struggles for breath. I can sense Albert's nervousness as he crouches beside me, but I ignore him.

"I found Papa's old hunting rifle," Florien goes on when he's recovered a bit. "I saw the German soldier at the end of our street and shot at him. I didn't aim to kill him. I just wanted to scare him and make him go home."

I blink hard and stare at my little brother. "It was you who shot at the soldier?"

"Yes. After they took Papa, I was too scared to give myself up. I convinced myself that they wouldn't shoot the hostages, but they did. I killed Papa."

The effort of his long admission exhausts Florien and he closes his eyes. The shock of what he's told me has stopped my tears. His childish attempt to scare the entire German army into going home led to Papa's death and flooded him in guilt—and then I deserted him. While I was traveling to exotic places and believing that it's easy to tell good from bad, Florien was back here struggling with horrific guilt and crushing loneliness. My refuge was escape, while his was the only friends he could find—the thugs who admire German power and believe that Belgium should be split in two. Suddenly Florien's anger, drinking and extreme politics make sense. They are all attempts to hide from himself and what he has to live with.

"I'm cold," he murmurs.

"He's going into shock," Albert says, draping his uniform jacket over him.

"It's not your fault," I say, stroking my brother's forehead. It feels cold. "You didn't know what you were doing. It was the Germans who killed Papa."

Florien opens his eyes and looks up at me. "Was it?" he asks.

"Of course it was. You didn't even mean to hurt the soldier. It was the Germans who took the hostages and killed them. You are innocent."

A broad smile forms on his face, making him look years younger. "Thank you," he says and closes his eyes.

Chapter 20

Going Home—May 12, 1917

Now we really have to go," Albert says. He drags the body of the German officer across the docks and pushes it off the edge into the water. Several Belgian workers are standing some distance away in the shadows, but they don't interfere.

"He's still alive," I say, feeling Florien's pulse. The bloodstain on his chest isn't getting any larger, so I think the bleeding's slowed. "We have to get him out."

"It's not long until dawn and the plane won't wait," Albert says.

I think he's about to suggest we leave Florien, so I give him a look that makes it obvious that's not an option. Albert steps forward and lifts Florien onto his back as gently as possible.

We stagger away from the dock, but I know there's no way we can walk to Koolkerke in time. Already a narrow strip of pale sky is showing along the eastern horizon, and Koolkerke is about a twenty-minute walk—even without Albert carrying Florien.

One of the watching Belgian workers moves tentatively toward us. I hope he's not going to try to stop us. I don't think I have the energy left to fight.

"Where are you going?" the man asks.

"Koolkerke," I reply.

He takes a long look at Albert with Florien on his back, turns and runs into a nearby building. He returns moments later pushing a flat two-wheeled cart. "Put him on this," he says. "It will be faster."

Albert lays Florien on the cart, takes up the handles and heads off.

"Thank you," I say to the man, before I follow Albert.

Leaving the dockyard is easy. A number of walking wounded are heading for the hospital, so we just join the crowd. My nurse's uniform helps us blend in, and no one stops us. Once we're out the gate, we take the road to Koolkerke and leave the others behind.

Flashes begin to appear in the dark sky to the north, and the deep rumble of heavy guns signals the beginning of the naval attack on the Zeebrugge lock.

"That's the navy for you," Albert says. "Late as usual."

We haven't gone more than a few hundred yards before I see a cyclist coming toward us.

"Manon," Amelie shouts as she approaches, "where have you been?"

"It's a long story," I say, grinning happily at the sight of my friend. "Is the plane at Koolkerke?"

"It is, but the pilot is nervous. He won't wait long."

"Cycle back as fast as you can and tell him that we're coming. He has to wait."

Amelie nods and pedals off.

"Just as well I grew up on a farm," Albert says, increasing his pace. "Lots of practice pushing carts of animal feed around."

I walk beside the cart holding Florien's hand. He's still unconscious, but his breathing is regular and he groans at every bump in the road. His face looks relaxed and young. I think about what I'll do when we reach the plane, and about whether I've made the right decision. Should I have taken Florien straight to the hospital and sent Albert to the plane on his own? I couldn't think of a way to explain how a bullet hole from a German pistol got in my brother, especially after a dead officer is dragged from the canal.

It's light enough to see the silhouette of the plane by the time we reach Amelie at the side of the road. The machine is long and sleek with a rounded nose and two engines. The pilot is sitting in the open cockpit beneath the upper wing, and the gunners' positions in the nose and behind the pilot are open. The engines are running.

"A Caudron," Albert says. "A French machine. Good piece of work." He's breathing heavily from the effort of pushing Florien's cart.

"We must hurry," Amelie says as we reach her. "Manon, you climb in behind the pilot. Albert can go in the nose."

"I'm not going," I say.

She stares at me. "You must. It's too dangerous for you to stay."

"Everything is dangerous in war," I say. "With a German bullet in him, Florien will be in much more danger if he stays. And he will get better medical attention in London. Albert saw as much as I did in the dockyard, and he can pass on my photographs." I hand him my camera, which he accepts with a nod.

"You can't—" Amelie wants to argue, but she stops when she sees how determined I am. "All right," she agrees reluctantly.

The three of us lift Florien over the fence and carry him across the field. As we lift him into the position behind the pilot, his eyes flicker open.

"Where am I?" he asks.

"On your way home," I say.

He nods weakly and smiles. "You're a good sister."

"I know," I agree, leaning forward to kiss him on the cheek. "Just get better."

"It's almost full daylight," the pilot shouts back from the cockpit. "We can't hang around all day."

I jump down as Albert climbs into the gunner's position in the nose. "Thank you, Manon!" he yells.

I suddenly think of something and jump onto the nose wheel so I'm level with Albert.

"Do me a favor?"

Albert nods.

"Try to get a message to a tunneller I know. His name's Alec Shorecross. Last I heard, he was in 169 Tunnelling Company. Tell him I'm all right and I miss him."

Albert grins. "I'll pass on your message. You look after yourself. And thank you."

"Come on, come on," the pilot urges.

I jump back down onto the grass. The engine note increases. On an impulse, I yell to Albert, "Tell Alec I love him."

Albert laughs and gives me a thumbs-up. The plane begins to move and Amelie pulls me out of the way of the wing as it swings around. With a roar, the Caudron bounces across the field and drags itself into the air. There's still a battle raging over Zeebrugge and I hope it will distract the Germans so much that they won't notice a single plane flying west.

Amelie and I head back to the road and toward Damme. "I'm looking forward to hearing the story of your adventures last night," she says. "Pieter will be interested as well. He's been making contacts with people he's certain he can trust. He'll have to get false identity papers and go underground, but everything should be ready for the next task." She looks at me. "It was very brave of you to stay."

I shrug and smile. "I knew you wouldn't be able to manage on your own," I say as we walk beside the canal. "There's a lot of work to be done."

AUTHOR'S NOTE

While Manon, Pieter and Amelie are fictitious, the organization they worked for, La Damme Blanche, was real. Throughout the First World War, dozens of brave girls and women collected and passed the Allies information on German troop movements and activities in Belgium. The most famous member of the group was Gabrielle Petit, who, as Manon tells Albert, was executed in 1916, and whose statute now stands in the Place Saint-Jean in Brussels.

Several airfields in Belgium were used by the Germans to launch their zeppelin raids on Britain. The zeppelins were a terrifying sight, but they did little real damage, and by the middle of the war the British had developed effective ways to combat them. The German response was to turn to their Gotha bombers, which began raiding in May 1917. The Gothas were more effective, but the Germans never had enough of them to make a difference.

The giant bomber that Manon sees arriving at Gontrode on her first mission is a Zeppelin-Staaken R.VI. Some versions had five engines, a crew of seven and the wingspan of a B-29 Superfortress, the largest bomber in the Second World War. Only eighteen R.VIs were built, but they could carry enormous bombs and prefigured the massive bombing raids of the Second World War. They were used in in Russia in the summer of 1917, and began raiding Britain in the fall of that same year. I have moved the arrival of an R.VI at Gontrode a bit forward in time so that Manon can see one.

The German U-boat campaign of 1917 came close to starving Britain out of the war, and numerous attempts to bomb the pens at Bruges or the canals that led from there to Zeebrugge and Ostend were carried out. Zeebrugge was heavily shelled on the morning on May 12, although the attack began two hours late and failed to destroy the locks. A more famous attempt in 1918, which included a landing party and sunken block ships, also failed. Eventually, the U-boat menace was undone by convoys, aircraft, depth charges and Q-ships.

There are very few books about spying in the First World War, and most of them focus on Mata Hari and spying in Britain. An internet search for Gabrielle Petit will bring up several biographies. Zeppelin Nights by Jerry White gives a good sense of life in London while the zeppelins and Gothas flew overhead.

Glossary

Boche—Slang for a German soldier or pilot.

Jan Breydel and Pieter de Coninck—The leaders of a fourteenth-century uprising against the French. There's a statue to them in the main square in Bruges.

Caudron—The Caudron R4 was a successful three-seater French reconnaissance aircraft used in 1916 and 1917. Its streamlined design was ahead of its time.

Charlie Chaplin—A famous silent movie comedian who made dozens of immensely popular films from 1914 onward.

Dinant—A Belgian town where 674 civilians, including many women and children, were massacred when the Germans invaded on August 23 and 24, 1914.

Directorate of Military Intelligence—A war agency formed in 1916 from the British Secret Service. Department 6 (also called MI6) was in charge of collecting intelligence from agents overseas.

F.E.2b—A British fighter/bomber used throughout the First World War in various roles. Its engine was at the back, pushing the plane forward so that the gunner in the front had a clear line of fire.

Flare—A device producing a very bright flame, used to signal or to illuminate the landscape. Flares of many kinds and colours were used in the First World War.

Flemish Movement—A political movement dedicated to achieving greater rights and sometimes independence for the Flemish-speaking areas of Belgium. During the First World War, the German occupiers encouraged the Flemish Movement as a way of disrupting Belgian resistance to the invasion.

Fokker—A German aircraft manufacturer, famous for the Fokker Eindecker, which devastated the more primitive British planes in 1915 and early 1916. This phase of the war is the setting for Wings of War.

Fritz—A slang term for a German soldier or pilot.

Front lines—The trenches closest to the enemy.

Gotha—A large twin-engine German bomber that was used in different variants throughout the First World War. In 1917, it largely took over the bombing of England from the vulnerable zeppelins.

Handley Page—This bomber was the British equivalent of the Gotha and was used to bomb many German targets in Belgium during the war.

Hangar—A large shed used for storing aircraft.

Homing pigeons—Pigeons that have been trained to return home once released somewhere else. They were used extensively for sending messages in the First World War and even in the Second World War. Recently, the mummified remains of a Second World War homing pigeon, with the coded message still attached to its leg, was found in a chimney in England.

Hussar—Light horseman used as cavalry early in the First World War and later as regular infantry.

Max Immelmann—The first German flying ace (fifteen victories) in the war. He was shot down in June 1916 by an F.E.2b.

Kodak Vest Pocket Camera—The world's first compact camera. It was 1 inch (2.5 cm) thick, 2.5 inches (6 cm) wide, and only 4.75 inches (12 cm) high. Because it could easily fit in a uniform pocket, it became immensely popular with soldiers, who were not supposed to take cameras to war. Many of the surviving photographs of the war were taken with these extraordinary cameras.

La Dame Blanche—The White Lady was the resistance and spy network in Belgium during the First World War. It took its name from an old legend that predicted the fall of the German monarchy would be announced by the appearance of a woman dressed all in white. By the end of the war, there were thirteen hundred agents in the network, many of them women and young girls.

Leuven—A Belgian town taken by the Germans in August 1914. German soldiers set fire to the town's world-famous university library, destroying 230,000 books, at least a thousand of which had been printed before 1501. The library was rebuilt and restocked after the First World War, but it was again destroyed, with the loss of one million books, in the Second World War.

Lewis gun—A British machine gun with a drum of ammunition that clipped onto the top. It was light and simple enough to be mounted on early fighter planes.

Percheron—A breed of large draft horses. One legend has it that they are descended from horses that were sent to reinforce Julius Caesar's legions in Gaul more than two thousand years ago.

Q-ships—Merchant ships that were fitted with hidden guns so they could lure a submarine onto the surface and then destroy it.

Red Cross—A humanitarian organization that was founded in 1863 in Switzerland and has won the Nobel Peace Prize three times. During the First World War, the Red Cross provided communication pathways between countries at war and supplied parcels of clothing and food to prisoners.

Royal Flying Corps (RFC)—The British air force in the First World War. It became the Royal Air Force (RAF) in 1918.

Somme—A huge allied offensive that took place between July 1 and November 18, 1916.

Tunnellers—The men who dug tunnels and placed huge explosive mines beneath enemy trenches and strongpoints in the First World War. Alec, who is much in Manon's thoughts, is a tunneller. His story is told in Dark Terror.

Tyburn—The site of public hangings outside London from 1196 to 1783.

U-boats—Short for *Unterseeboot* ("undersea boat"), U-boat is the name given to all German submarines in both world wars.

Waterloo—Battle in 1815 that ended the Napoleonic Wars. The British and Prussian armies, commanded by Wellington and Blucher respectively, defeated the French army led by Napoleon.

Zeppelin—The huge airships that were used by the Germans as bombers in the days before planes could carry enough weight. They were slow, vulnerable to being blown off course and easy to set fire to (since they were filled with flammable hydrogen). The Zeppelin company also built planes, including the giant bomber that Manon sees at Gontrode.

If you enjoyed **A Dangerous Game**, you might enjoy the Caught in Conflict Collection. Here's sample of one of them:

Flames of the Tiger: Berlin 1945

"...this book, like Wilson's And in the Morning, presents a compelling and thoughtful story of war that should appeal to a wide range of readers" Quill & Quire

Chapter 1

Dieter peered over the lip of the ditch. The acrid smell of burning fuel irritated his nose. Across the field, a burning Tiger tank lay stark and black against the sunset's fragile colours, its long cannon pointing uselessly at the heavens. Deep red flames licked upward from pools of spilled fuel, and a column of heavy, roiling smoke rose in the still evening air. A dead man lay on the scorched grass nearby, and another, his charred body arched in a final agony, was trapped half out of the tank's open hatch. Slowly Dieter scanned the field for signs of life—there were none.

He let out a long breath and relaxed.

"Is it all right?" an urgent whisper came from behind him.

The boy slithered back down the slope until he was lying beside his sister. "I think so. There's a tank in the field, but everyone's dead."

Dieter looked up at the sky. The pink of the setting sun on the thunderheads competed with the reflected glow of the burning village the pair had passed through that afternoon.

"This is as good a place as any to spend the night," Dieter said. "If the clouds bring rain, we'll cross to those trees or shelter under the tank if it's stopped burning by then."

Dieter extracted his water bottle and took a sip. His mouth was dry, and the desire to gulp the bottle empty was powerful, but he forced himself to stop and pass it to Greta.

"Just a sip," he warned.

"I know, I know," Greta replied. "Stop nagging." She took a sip and passed the bottle back. Dieter screwed on the top and replaced it in his pack. He pulled out a loaf of stale black bread, the last of the food Uncle Walter had given them two days before. It was coarse and unpleasant, but better than the sawdust-filled stuff they'd had in Berlin. In the long run, the bread would make Dieter's thirst worse, but he promised himself another sip of water when it was finished. He broke the loaf in half and handed a piece to Greta.

She groaned. "I'd give anything for a cream pastry, loaded with jam," she said wistfully.

"Don't torture yourself," Dieter advised as he sullenly chewed. "This is all we've got. Besides, you never liked cream pastries."

"I did so," Greta responded indignantly.

One of his sister's most irritating habits was an ability to rewrite the past to suit her mood. Dieter had long ago learned that he couldn't win an argument when Greta had convinced herself of something, so he let it go and ate in silence.

Despite his own advice, Dieter couldn't stop his mind drifting back to better days. It was something he often did. His father had called it daydreaming and said it was a waste of time, but many times recently, Dieter's memories had helped him get through the present. A good daydream was a treasure. Dieter's surroundings faded, time slowed, and the past opened up in his mind like a movie. Sometimes when it was happening, he felt as if he were two people—the one who could sit at his school desk or walk or even carry on a simple conversation, and the one who was reliving some wonderful event.

Right now, while the surface Dieter chewed a mouthful of stale bread by the glow of a burning tank, the real Dieter was thirteen years old and sitting at the formal dining room table in the family apartment on the Charlottenburger. It was three years ago, Christmas Eve dinner 1941. The German armies were sweeping victoriously over the Russian Steppes and everyone thought the war was as good as won. Elsa still cooked and cleaned for the family, and the curtains over the long windows didn't need to be closed against the bombers. Dieter could stand at the windows and look out over the Tiergarten to the distant buildings of the zoo. He loved the zoo, the view out the window and the ornate high-ceilinged rooms of the apartment, but his favourite thing in the whole world was the dining room table.

~~~~~

The shine on the table was deep and magical, a pond with cool liquid depths that Dieter's imagination could reach into to pull out all manner of strange life. But it was solid—solid enough to support the gleaming silverware and carved crystal glasses. And the tureens and servers and plates, piled high with steaming potatoes, vegetables and meat.

Glorious smells filled the room—the warm, rich odour of ham and turkey, the sharp, slightly sour smell of cabbage. And wonderful tastes were there for the sampling—the sweetness of his mother's famous strudels, the saltiness of the soup, the fresh crispness of a Waldorf salad.

Dieter's father, Ernst, sat at the head of the table, looking every inch the family patriarch with his old-fashioned bushy moustache. At the foot sat Dieter's mother, Eva, resplendent in lace. To one side were Dieter and his little sister, Greta. On the table beside her, glinting in the candlelight, lay her most precious possession, her flute. It had been a present for her eighth birthday the previous March, and it went everywhere with her. All year, she had practiced with a devotion that bordered on fanaticism, and even Dieter had to admit that she was getting quite good. Ernst allowed the flute to be brought to the table on condition that Greta play them a tune after the meal.

Opposite Greta was Dieter's twenty-year-old brother, Reinhard, looking splendid in his immaculate new SS uniform. Reinhard took after their mother. With his blond hair, high cheekbones, sharp nose and firm chin, he was the ideal Aryan man. Dieter wished he was tall and fair like Reinhard, but he had inherited his father's softer features, round face, brown hair and short stature.

Reinhard and Ernst were discussing the government.

"But you must admit, Father," Reinhard said, "Hitler has done such a lot for Germany. The punishing provisions that the British, French and Americans forced on us in the Versailles Treaty after the Great War were crushing our country. Hitler stood up to them and they backed down. Our economy is secure, there is work for everyone, and we see no more of the street violence that the Communists caused a decade ago. The displaced German communities in Austria, Czechoslovakia and Poland have been brought back into a nation that is being steadily purified of the undesirable elements that have been holding us back for so long. The war is almost won. It is a new age. How can you not see that it is better than the old world you grew up in?"

"I agree that the Nazis have achieved a lot. Versailles was iniquitous, our economy was a dreadful mess, and I have no more love than you for Jews and Communists, but do not dismiss the values of my world so glibly. I know that my family was privileged. We had estates in East Prussia, servants and aristocratic friends in very high places."

"And dogs and ponies," Greta interrupted excitedly. "That's what I would have loved. Can we get a dog?"

Ernst laughed. "We live in an apartment, and you probably want a wolfhound."

"Oh yes. One of those big hairy ones with the long noses."

"It wouldn't be fair on the dog, Greta. Those animals need a lot of exercise. More than the occasional walk in the Tiergarten.

"And I accept a lot of what you say, Reinhard. Much of my world is gone, lost in the inflation of the twenties and the stock market crash of nineteen twenty-nine, but it was doomed long before that. The trenches of the Kaiser's war destroyed my world, but there were some worthwhile things left. We had standards: we believed it was important to behave in a certain way, to show respect to others and to comport ourselves in a civilized, sophisticated manner. This is what separated us from the rabble. And you forget that ten years ago, it was not just the Communists who rioted in the streets. The people who now sit in our government, and whom you admire so much, began by smashing people's heads in street battles. They are vulgar, crude and lower-class. To have them in charge is a reversal of the structure of any civilized society.

"When Hitler won the election in 1932, I was convinced that the Nazi government wouldn't last six months. I was wrong there, and I have to admit that they have done our country some good, but I cannot believe that such a bunch of boorish rabble-rousers can be good in the long term."

"Oh, Father," Reinhard said, "you are so old-fashioned. You have to change with the times. Germany is great again, and it wasn't class and elegant manners that got us here, it was action.

"If you want to see the real lower classes, look at the Russians. The Panzers and the Luftwaffe are unbeatable in the east—every battle produces hordes of Russian prisoners. These Slavs are hopeless. One good German soldier is worth a whole platoon of them. If it wasn't for the Jewish Communist political officers warping their simple minds and pointing machine guns at their backs to force them to attack, the war would be over by now. Moscow would have fallen and we would be marching through Red Square taking the lebensraum, the living space our destiny demands. Soon, solid Aryan stock will populate Russia."

Ernst sat silent for a long moment. Dieter sensed a change in the room. He fiddled nervously with his fork. At length, Ernst went on, but his voice was slower and his tone more serious. "And what would you do with the people already there?"

"Well," Reinhard sat back and launched into his favourite topic. "They will be resettled—after we get rid of all the Jews and Communists, of course."

"What do you mean by 'get rid of'?" Dieter's father's voice was quiet, but his words cut through Reinhard's enthusiastic tirade. Dieter felt the tension mount. Where was this conversation going? Ernst and Reinhard stared at each other. Then Reinhard smiled. "There's no need to worry about them," he said. "They can work— for the greater good."

"As slave labor?"

Reinhard shrugged.

"Slave labor and then what?" Ernst persisted.

"Then nothing. They won't be allowed to reproduce, so they will simply die out."

"Simply die out!" Ernst's voice rose in anger. "Good God, man, even Slavs and Jews are human. What you are suggesting is barbaric."

Everyone else at the table sat in silence. Even Greta had nothing to say as her gaze moved nervously between her father and her brother. Only Reinhard seemed composed and comfortable. His smile didn't falter.

"You are wrong there, Father," he said. "They are the barbarians. History proves that it is we, the true Aryan stock, who are destined to rule. We would do so already if our genes had not been contaminated by inferior blood and if the Jewish Conspiracy was not so powerful. My generation's task is to purify the German nation. To get rid of the contaminants, to return the Aryan stock to the purity that made it great in the past. Imagine it—a single race from the Asian steppes to the Atlantic coast! What a great day that will be. It is a difficult task requiring fortitude and persistence, but it must be done. The future demands it."

"Please," Eva pleaded. "It's Christmas."

"I'm sorry, but I cannot let this go." Ernst's voice was barely above a whisper. He addressed his apology to his wife, but he never took his eyes off his son.

"Reinhard," Ernst continued. "The future demands nothing. Do not use historical necessity as an excuse. The things we see around us and think so important are mere flotsam swept along by the river of time. We can no more shape the future to fit our petty desires than we can stop time. If it were possible to create the future, do you think the world would have gone through madness and horror I saw in the Kaiser's war?

"In my war, I saw lines of men fall before our machine guns like long grass in the wind. It was a futile, horrible waste, but at least the men were soldiers, doing what soldiers have always had to do and paying the price soldiers have always paid. You are talking about controlling the lives of millions of civilians. We may not like them, or want them to live beside us, but they are human beings, and no one, however much semi-mystical nonsense they invent to support their views, is entitled to turn an entire people into slaves."

Dieter's fork clattered onto his plate with a noise that made Greta jump. Ernst ignored the interruption.

"You asked me earlier, Reinhard, if I could not see that your world is much better than mine. I see good things in it, but there is neither class nor compassion underlying it. Therefore, there are no checks against going too far. My generation made mistakes—some horrible ones, I admit that—but when I hear you talk of such things, I truly fear where these men you admire so much will lead us.

"You are my son. I have watched you grow from a baby, and I love you. But your mind has become twisted by self-centred demagogues spouting rubbish passed off as thought. You are an adult and must make your own decisions, for better or worse, but I will not have such claptrap at my dinner table."

Reinhard's smile had vanished as his father spoke, replaced by a look of grim determination. Now he rose, pushing his heavy chair back with a long grating sound. Dieter could see the muscles in his jaw clenched in anger. "You are a fool, Ernst Hammer," Reinhard said. "The future is mine. You may rail against it, but it will swallow you as easily as it will the Slav hordes. You may not care if the family is dragged down with you, but I do. I shall do as you ask and bite my tongue in your little kingdom for their sakes. But remember that the large world outside is mine."

Reinhard strode toward the dining room door. With his hand on the latch, he turned and looked straight at Dieter.

"Dieter," he said, "be careful not to get stuck in this old man's past. The future is yours, too, and you must embrace your place in it or be crushed."

As Reinhard's footsteps echoed down the hallway, Dieter was a turmoil of emotions—he was being asked to choose between the two people he admired most in the world: the big brother who had taught him to play football and taken him fishing in the city's many canals and rivers, and the father who had taught him to both show and expect respect and told him stories of the different world he had grown up in.

Dieter felt he was being torn apart. He yearned for the simple, colourful past his father talked of, but he couldn't deny the seductive attraction of the dynamic world being created around him by people like his brother.

Slowly Dieter realized that everyone was looking at him. They seemed to be demanding a decision. Why did he have to be drawn into this? Why wouldn't everyone just leave him alone?

Tears pooled in the corners of Dieter's eyes. To hide them, he violently pushed back his chair and fled to his room, where he lay weeping on his bed.

Flames of the Tiger and the other eight stories in the Caught in Conflict Collection are available as both eBooks and Paperbacks on Amazon.

Other Titles

Shot at Dawn
Allan McBride has fought in some of the First World War's bloodiest battles. He has seen his comrades, and his best friend, killed. But tonight he waits in a shed outside Amiens, accused of desertion, to discover if dawn will bring a last-minute reprieve—or execution by firing squad.

"...the powerful writing and strong characters will grip readers from beginning to end."—Quill & Quire

Graves of Ice
Thrilled at being a part of such a great adventure, George Chambers volunteers to join Sir John Franklin's expedition in search of the elusive Northwest Passage. But as the ice traps both *Erebus* and *Terror* in a desolate, frozen landscape, the explorers' search for the fabled passage deteriorates to a grim struggle to avoid death by starvation, freezing or scurvy. Eventually, only George remains alive searching vainly for a rescuing sail on the horizon.

"...a compelling story...a haunting story that keeps the reader riveted."—CM Magazine

Lost Cause *(The SEVEN Series)*
Steve travels to Spain and uncovers his late grandfather's involvement in the Spanish Civil War. Followed by a sequel, **Broken Arrow** and a prequel, **The Missing Skull**

"I had to force myself to take a break for food and sleep. I just wanted to keep reading."—ALSA's Top Ten review program

And in the Morning: Somme 1916
"And in the Morning joins other outstanding novels about the First World War—an invaluable resource for libraries and classrooms."—Jeffrey Canton, Quill & Quire

Four Steps to Death: Stalingrad 1942
"This absorbing, well-crafted tale...is a haunting description of the tragedy and irony of war...In this vivid narrative, the awful

cacophony of war comes to life...the skilled author succeeds without moralistic preaching in highlighting the harsh reality, the utter misery, and the heartbreak of war in this intricate but fascinating book."—VOYA

Lost in Spain: The Spanish Civil War 1936

"Wilson offers a unique perspective on this fascinating era...even minor characters are brought to life."—Library Journal

Flags of War: Shiloh 1862

"...action-filled, tightly written prose. Realistic battle scenes illustrate the senselessness of war...the story offers a fresh take on the conflict - the idea of Canada as refuge for fugitive slaves and the irony of how it was nearly drawn into the war on the side of the South."—Albany Public Library, NY

Battle Scars: Libby Prison 1865

"Readable and exciting."—Booklist

Germania: The Roman Empire 9 A.D.

"This riveting, haunting tale will leave readers clamouring for more."—Best Books

Where Soldiers Lie: India 1857

"This is an absolutely terrific book...Never lagging with a credible hero and an exotic setting...The pacing is flawless."—Geoffrey Bilson Award for Historical Fiction Jury Citation

"The tension and action of the battle and the intense danger of the escape from the massacre will keep readers turning these pages."—Quill & Quire

The Alchemist's Dream

In the fall of 1669, the Nonsuch returns to London with a load of fur from Hudson Bay. It brings something else, too—the lost journal from Henry Hudson's tragic search for a passage to Cathay in 1611. In the hands of a greedy sailor, the journal is merely an object to sell. But for Robert Bylot—a once-great maritime explorer—the book is a painful reminder of a past he'd rather forget. As Bylot relives his memories of a plague-ridden city, of the mysterious alchemist John Dee, and of mutiny in the frozen wastes of Hudson Bay, an age-old mystery is both revealed and solved. Set against the thrilling backdrop of the quest for the Northwest

Passage, The Alchemist's Dream is a riveting tale of exploration, ambition, and betrayal. Also available in an expanded edition that includes extracts from Hudson's journal, **The Final Alchemy**.

"In this engrossing historical adventure, John Wilson paints a vivid picture of a bygone era involving Henry Hudson's fateful search for the elusive Northwest Passage, an alchemist, mysterious passengers, and enigmatic maps. The Alchemist's Dream fascinates from start to finish."—Governor General's Award jury citation.

A Soldier's Sketchbook: The Illustrated First World War Diary of R. H. Rabjohn

A unique First World War diary, illustrated with more than a hundred stunning pencil and ink sketches, for children learning history and also for adults interested in a new perspective on the war and authentic wartime artefacts.

"The extracts from the diary describe intimate wartime experiences of death and destruction in gruesomely dispassionate terms...it's a story of unmitigated horror, highlighting more than any textbook the futility of war...This unique compilation of firsthand impressions of the Great War will be a valuable resource for adults and teens with an interest in this turning point in world history."—Kirkus Starred Review

"The excellent and succinct text . . . provides context for Rabjohn's short diary entries, many of which merely scratch the surface of the suffering he experienced during his time at war."—Starred Review, Quill & Quire

Norman Bethune: A Brief Biography

As a young man, Norman Bethune served as a stretcher-bearer in the First World War. The experience left him with the dedication and passion to lead crusades to find a cure for tuberculosis, to introduce universal health care in Canada, and to introduce mobile blood transfusion units to save wounded soldier's lives on the battlefield. He served with the Republican armies during the Spanish Civil War and in China where he died of blood poisoning in 1939. Because of his left wing politics, Bethune was ignored for decades in his home country. His childhood home in Gravenhurst, Ontario sees large numbers of visitors each year, although a majority are tourists from China where he is revered as a hero for his work with Mao's army in its fight against the Japanese. Regardless of politics, Bethune deserves to be more highly regarded everywhere for his lifelong struggle against injustice and suffering wherever he encountered it.

"I couldn't put the Bethune story down...It is an inspirational tale as well as a historically important one."—Times-Colonist

"...John Wilson makes the private man come alive...[a] gripping story of a larger-than-life Canadian hero."—Quill & Quire

John Franklin: A Brief Biography

Sir John Franklin was many things in his life: an officer in the great naval battles of Copenhagen and Trafalgar; governor of Van Diemen's Land; an explorer from Australia to the Arctic, but it is for his mysterious death and the deaths of all 128 of his crew that he is remembered today. The mystery of the disappearance of the Franklin Expedition to the Northwest Passage has captivated thousands in the 174 years since his men buried Franklin in an unknown grave in the frozen land that kept calling him back. For most of that time only a handful of graves, scattered bones, fragments of debris and Inuit stories have fuelled the speculation as to what killed them all. Now, the wrecks of both of Franklin's ships have been found, preserved in the frigid waters off King William Island, and may contain answers that have been sought for generations. This is the story of the man whose name will forever be associated with the greatest tragedy in Arctic exploration history.

"This book, admirable in its succinctness...is the best life of Franklin yet produced...there could be no better introduction to the life and journeys of Franklin than Wilson's...wonderfully engaging book."—Russell Potter, Arctic Book Review

An *"...excellent overview, the reader is left with an appreciation of the enormous task early exploration of the Arctic represented...a first rate story and a very useful addition to our understanding and appreciation of an important and unique segment of Canadian history. Highly Recommended."*—CM Magazine

Heretic: The Heretic's Secret book 1
In the style of Bernard Cornwell, The Heretic's Secret Trilogy is a rollicking historical adventure set during the bloody 13th century wars against the Cathar Heretics of Languedoc. When the armoured knights of Pope Innocent III swept south in 1209, most thought they would be gone by summer's end but, led by the fanatical Arnaud Aumery and the ambitious Simon de Montfort, they stayed for three fiery decades. In that time they slaughtered thousands of Cathars, burned countless towns and castles, destroyed a thriving country that rivalled France in power and culture, and created the foundations for the shape of western Europe we recognize today. John and Peter enjoy arguing about their differing views of the world. Peter sees the Church and an unquestioning acceptance of God's word as the way to salvation. John sees developing an understanding of the wonder of the world around him as a way of becoming closer to God. As the chaos of war erupts around them, the friendly differences of childhood demand that they take sides. Troubled by mysterious visions, Peter seeks refuge in the Church and becomes an assistant to the militant Aumery. Repelled by the horror he sees around him, John finds himself drawing closer to the persecuted Cathar heretics. As the brutal holy war expands and the flames of the Inquisition spread, Peter and John find themselves on opposite sides of a dangerous search for a secret that may have the power to change the world. **Quest** and **Rebirth** follow John and Peter's thrilling adventures to their heart-rending conclusion.

"...a brave book, an unsettling book, and one that is very much needed at this time."—The Globe and Mail

"...an astonishingly nuanced and masterfully told story..."—Quill & Quire

The Third Act *(soon to be a major live-action movie)*
The Third Act deals with the intercultural struggles faced by Chinese students studying in North America in the present day and by an American playwright, Neil Peterson, caught up in the Nanjing Massacre of 1937. The contemporary story focuses on three Chinese friends (Tone, Pike and Theresa) who grapple in their own ways with the pressure to succeed in an unfamiliar culture. The historical tale concerns Peterson's effort to find his literary voice

and save the woman he loves amidst the chaos and horror of the fall of Nanjing in the Second Sino-Japanese War. The two stories are tied together by a play that Peterson attempted to write after his return to America. The students in the present day get caught up in putting on a performance of the missing third act of Peterson's play, and in doing so they are forced to confront their cultural and personal pasts and futures.

"I recommend The Third Act to students who enjoy both historical fiction and mystery novels. The novel has a strong, well-developed female character in Theresa...Highly Recommended."—CM Magazine

The Ruined City: book 1 of The Golden Mask *(The inspiration for the upcoming animated feature, Heroes of the Golden Mask)*
Howard is a lonely, geeky tenth-grader dealing with a father who's had some kind of breakdown, a flaky, overprotective mother and frightening waking dreams. Then he meets Cate, a strange girl who convinces him that he is an Adept, which means he can communicate through dreams with other dimensions and, under certain circumstances, travel between them. Howard discovers that our world is only one of several dimensions swirling in time and space, and that one of the others, peopled by unimaginably powerful monsters, is approaching Earth for the first time in millennia. The last time the dimensions coincided, our world was saved by the breaking of a powerful golden mask in the Bronze Age Chinese city of Sanxingdui. Together, Howard and Cate travel through time and space, meeting other Adepts and avoiding lurking monsters, in a quest to find the three fragments of the golden mask and prevent it from falling into the wrong hands.

"A tale of adventure and monsters, The Ruined City, with more than a nod to H.P. Lovecraft, should appeal to readers who enjoy a mystery and slimy monsters from another dimension. Highly Recommended."—CM Magazine

"An ambitious story...Fascinating."—Kirkus Reviews

Ghost Mountains and Vanished Oceans: North America from Birth to Middle Age *(new edition complete with the original maps and appendices included)*
This book is more than the story of how a continent formed over 4 billion years. Told in readable, entertaining prose and filled with

personal and geological anecdotes, Ghost Mountains and Vanished Oceans tells the story of our world and, in doing so, it tells our story. As the author puts it, "We are not just passengers on a dead piece of cosmic debris whirling through space; we are an integral part of an exceptional, dynamic system that produced both our earth and us."

"...a fascinating read for anyone interested in the planet on which we live and how it came to be as it is..."—Geoscience Canada

"...this book is a true, well-crafted page-turner...if you've ever wondered how the continents and the particular slab of rock you live on came about, you will love this book...Highly Recommended."— Amazon Reviewer

Find out more about these and other titles by John Wilson at www.johnwilson.com. All of John's 50 books are available through Amazon.